FLASHING LIGHTS

HAYLEY PERRIDGE

Order this book online at www.trafford.com
or email orders@trafford.com

Most Trafford titles are also available at major online book retailers.

Printed in the United States of America.

ISBN: 978-1-4269-9460-9 (sc)
ISBN: 978-1-4269-9461-6 (e)

Trafford rev. 10/31/2013

 www.trafford.com

North America & international
toll-free: 1 888 232 4444 (USA & Canada)
fax: 812 355 4082

"Go to sleep."

"Why should I?"

His brow furrowed. "Because it's 2 o'clock in the morning and you have school tomorrow."

"Well if you didn't insist on taking me for pizza I would have been counting sheep hours ago."

He sighed heavily, planting a soft kiss upon my forehead as he pulled me closer into his embrace. "Shut up…and go to sleep."

Grumbling quietly I buried my fingers into his t-shirt, wondering just how long he'd wait before leaving. It was then I smiled contently, closing my eyes and touching the tender spot upon my neck.

He'd wait forever, I already knew.

"Hey." Glancing upwards I glared into his eyes. "Hands off."

With a coy grin he chuckled, nuzzling his face into the juncture of my neck.

"Guess I couldn't help myself."

. . . .

Chapter 1

Opening my eyes I groaned, pulling the covers over my face as the sunlight escaped through my blinds. After a moments passing I threw the duvet back down, realising my odd looking room was now only occupying one. Rolling onto my back I began to wonder just what time he'd left last night. I did always try to wait up and find out, but I was usually so tired I dozed off as soon as my head hit the pillow. Though that's only what he'd told me; I sincerely hope I didn't snore. The window was always open in the mornings and I got sincerely annoyed when winter comes. Why with all these powers of his didn't he find a warmer way of leaving my bedroom, *without* me waking to find my toes beginning to be submitted to frostbite?

"Miya! Up! Now!"

Hearing my mother's military mouth I rolled my eyes and left my pit, placing my socked digits upon the wooden floor.

"Damn it!"

After I ended my cursing saga, I frowned down to whatever almost crushed my foot. Then my morning rage turned to a smile. I picked up a red glass ball, almost looking like a paperweight. Well, that's what my family thinks it is and that is how it shall stay. It's actually...well I'm not quite sure what is it but I know he likes to look at it while I finish my homework. He gave it to me. I do enjoy the fact that the red smoke inside moves around a lot, it gives me something to do whilst I listen to my mother wrestle my brother into the bath. He still doesn't know what personal hygiene is.

He never really told me what it does but I don't really mind, his face is cute when he's staring into it whilst I scribble down random answers in my geometry book.

"Miya, get your butt down here!"

"I'm coming already!" Placing the sphere back on my desk I left my room.

Many thoughts travel around my head as I descend the stairs. I wonder why the ball was on the floor instead of in its spot on my desk beside my laptop. He always watches it from there, sitting on my wheelie chair. He says he likes to keep moving. Can creatures of the night have ADHD?

"Argh, damn it again!"

My other foot felt missed out on the pain and so decided the have the imprint of my brother's fire engine etched on my skin.

"Watch your tongue young lady." I hear my mother's voice came from the kitchen, cluttering around as she usually does each stress filled morning.

"Tell that *thing* to put his stupid toys away. I could have broken my neck." I grumbled, plopping down on the floor as I walk into the battlefield known as our family eating area. Oh good, another day with burnt waffles.

"I am not a thing; I am the mighty Count Dracula!" My younger brother jumps at me dressed in some tacky cape and gummy fangs. I sigh, walking away from my hyped up sibling and towards the stool with the aroma of melting fat protruding my nose.

"Aren't you dressing up for school?" My mother places a glass of drinkable orange juice down in front of me. My mother is pretty I guess, long brownish hair and matching eyes; though you can see the dark circles around them. She denies their existence, but I often catch her poking at them in the bathroom mirror.

"You are kidding right? I'm in high school now; we don't walk around school looking like something out of the Rocky Horror Picture Show." I scowled, looking down to my plate of food that I shall feed to our trusty hound Peepers when she goes to wash last night's dishes.

"That's right; our baby girl is a junior now." My dad's voice echoed into the room, placing a kiss on my cheek as he scouts around for his morning newspaper, normally found in pieces within Peepers' basket.

"All grown up almost, I'll be picking out a wedding dress before I can blink." My mother sighed, droning into one of her 'my baby isn't a baby no more' speeches. How I despise those.

"Miya will look like a toad in a dress." My brother mumbled through his jam filled toast. "She looks like a toad in anything."

"You'll look like a *squashed* toad if you don't stop spewing crumbs all over me." I narrowed my eyes, a trait I've learnt from my grandmother. She can always give the look to send you as heavenly as an angel with an acceptance to Princeton.

"Stop arguing and I might just drive you to school." My father interrupts, placing his breakfast into the dog's bowl whilst placing a finger to his lips. Me and my brother both share the same giggling expression.

"That's if she gets dressed, now go!" My mother waves the kitchen towel in my face. I took time deciding on whether to be grateful I'd escaped the retched doom of stomaching rock hard waffles or annoyed that I was the one getting punished for something Jason had done, again.

My brother's name had always bothered me. Our names were so different, what on earth possessed my parents to name that brat after someone who sounds like they should be in a soap opera? Then again I wasn't too pleased to find out what my name meant.

"It's Japanese for rice valley." He'd told me, once bringing along a huge leather-bound book that looked like it belonged in the middle ages. I was profoundly put out after that, I wouldn't eat rice for at least a month afterwards.

I certainly don't look like a rice valley. For one my hair isn't soft and white, its black and wayward, kinking in all the wrong places for my liking. My eyes aren't some nice pretty colour either; they're a really funny shade of brown. I say funny because I'm sure one is lighter than the other, making me look like the kind of picture that some lazy kid couldn't be bothered to finish. Although I have to say I'm quite happy with my figure. Not so thin that bones stick out in all the wrongs places, but not so big that I don't shake the room as I walked in. I do have my mother's front though; it's quite normal. I think one is bigger than the other, something else to add to my list of unfinished factors.

"Come on Miya, you're gonna make everyone late!" My mother screamed from the bottom stairs, nudging me into placing on baggy jeans and a fitted hooded top, shoving on my sneakers as I grabbed my bag and zoomed out my bedroom.

As I sat in the car I realised I didn't really look like either of my parents. I turned my lolloping head to my dad in the driving seat. Sure he's got the same hair as me but its more straight, and there's a lot less of it. I don't think my parents are very happy with their trailing youth. He firmly denies the receding hairline, but he has the same bright blue eyes as my brother. I envy those gorgeous orbs set into that thick, ugly skull of his, probably thinking about something dumb as he smears fake blood onto his skin. My brother also has unruly black hair, but it suits him. Mother often says he'll be a heartbreaker when he grows up; personally I think he'll just break a few mirrors. "Great job sport." My dad beams to him through the rear-view mirror. "You look just like a vampire."

"If only you knew." I murmured, turning to face the moving world outside the window.

I always get dropped off last. I waited in the car for my brother to go scampering into 2nd grade, the school looking like an institution for the deviously wicked with the amount of costumes and pumpkins littered about the place. I've always hated Halloween, mainly because I always seemed to be in hospital that night. The nurses would come round dressed as witches and angels handing out candy and telling spooky stories. I wasn't allowed sugar, so I was given some replacement sweet that tasted like dank newspaper. Don't ask me how I came to that conclusion. With me being my shy 7 year old self, I withdrew from the activities, instead opting to pull out my sketchbook and drawing nice things, like bunnies and flowers. I didn't get why people wanted the living daylights sacred out of them, just for kicks. I couldn't understand it, my mum thought I was just being stupid, whilst my dad said I was just tired from my treatment. Either way I didn't believe in all that spooky crap. I do now.

As my dad drove me to the front gate of my school, I knew he wanted to talk to me. How? He had put the car in gear, leant back in his seat and gave a long and extremely deep sigh. I was looking through the window desperately for familiar faces, but I could feel his eyes boring into the back of my skull through the uncomfortable silence.

"Now before you go sweetheart, can I ask a favor?"

Sweetheart always gets me. I turned to my dad, face looking placid.

"I know you're not keen on all the Halloween stuff, but your mother and me are going to a party tonight..."

I knew exactly where this was going. Please don't say it...

"So can you take your little brother trick or treating?"

He said it. "Can't someone else take him?"

"Everyone we know will be at the party, even Grandma."

Of course she would, that lady is the scariest woman to walk the earth.

I must have frowned, because my dad leant over and placed his hands on my shoulders.

"I know it's not your idea of a good night but you only have to take him around the street, then you can come home and watch him get on a sugar high before falling asleep in the dog's bed."

He did that last year. Peepers wasn't impressed.

"Ok." I gave in, knowing I couldn't get around this even if I really. tried.

My dad smiled and kissed my forehead.

"You're a good girl." His shoulders relaxed. "You better go before you're late."

Nodding along to my dad's obvious advice I placed a strained smile upon my face before leaving the car.

"Find someone to tag along with you; it might get dark whilst you're still out!" He added, calling from the vehicle.

"Okay!" I cried, watching him wave and drive away down the street. As I walked past others kids heading towards the huge double doors of the school entrance, I sighed. This was going to be one crappy day.

"Sorry."

"No can do."

"Nuh uh."

"You guys suck!" I wailed, kicking my legs against the outside tarmac like a spoilt child.

"Like I care what you think of me right now." My friend Ella replied. "I have a hot date tonight and I'm not bailing out to go trick or treating with someone who doesn't even like Halloween and their kid brother."

"With who?" My other companion Emily asked, looking intensely curious.

"Bret of course." Ella swung her long blonde hair back over her shoulder, batting her big blue eyes. She looks like one of those models you see on the front of Vogue, but she's much nicer. Although a little snobby at times, she'll always come through for you. Well, apparently not *all* the time.

"Bret?" Emily yelped in excitement, jumping around in our customary gym kit like a hyperactive pixie. I wouldn't say she actually looks like one, but she is quite short and her curly brown hair bounces around in little pigtails like she was Tinkerbell's baby sister.

"He asked me yesterday over chit-chat." Ella replied, tying her hair back into a ponytail. "We're going to the movies for a scary flick."

Just so you know, chit-chat is our jargon for Internet messaging. Ella came up with it; thinking Internet messaging was too nerdy for us to say.

"What, so you can pretend to be scared and cling onto his arm to make him feel big and strong?"

Here comes the voice of reason. Resident user of common sense and President of all that is sane. Bending down to where I sat upon the floor in stupid looking shorts my best friend Sophie rolled her green eyes, tucking a piece of short black hair behind her ear. I had to smile.

"Hey he's cute!" Ella replied, jumping up and down on the spot to keep warm. "Why shouldn't I score on the scariest night of the year?"

"Argh, you sound just like a guy when you say that." Sophie answered, less than impressed. "Anyways I would come with you Mimi, but I have a dinner party with the tweevil's side of the family."

Although the damn nickname has stuck for the past 11 years, I do admire Sophie. Her mother died when she was little and a few years later her dad remarried. I remember being at the wedding with her as a bridesmaid; with a drip hanging out of my arm. I don't think her stepmother was too happy to see a bag of Saline in the wedding album. The 'tweevils' as she so lovingly calls them are her stepsisters. Both spoilt and both more fake than their hair extensions, Sophie is a true saint to be able to put up with them; then again she just wants her dad to be happy. Either way, she can't get out of a tweevils arrangement, so that just leaves Emily.

"So what can't you come with me?" I asked, looking up to the brunette with my most angelic look. It didn't work.

"My family have taken a stand to rebel against the holiday, my dad says it's materialistic and all about money so we've decided not to open the door after I get back from school."

Emily's family is a little insane. Her parents were both hippies back in the day, they met at a 'Save the endangered Red Cockroach' protest and fell in a groovy kind of love. It's safe to say they're a happy family; it's always fun to go round there. They have fair-trade bananas in a bowl by the front door. Ok, so I can forgive Emily and Sophie, but Ella is a different matter.

"So you're going to ditch your friend for a guy?" I pouted.

"Yep." Came her short, sharp reply. "It's not like you're in dire need here."

"Gee, thanks."

Whilst I wallowed in the misery that was my life, I noticed something on the other side of the school fence. Our sports area was next to a busy street so it was usual for people to walk by, though who I saw wasn't exactly normal in that aspect.

There he was standing in all his glory, looking right back at me with a smile. This day couldn't get any more messed up. I bolted up so fast Sophie fell backwards whilst I continued running towards the edge of the playground.

"Hey, where are you going?" Ella called after me, though I tried to ignore her the very best I could.

"I'll never understand why you have to do sports in the winter, in shorts." He spoke as I stood opposite him, with just the chicken wire separating us.

"It's not winter, it's fall." I replied, though I could feel my knees starting to knock together. "What are you doing here?"

Chapter 2

Forget all the rumors and old folk tales you've heard about vampires, they're not true. In fact they're quite absurd when you think about them. Alex explained all this to me just after we met; he found it ludicrously comical that Buffy the Vampire Slayer would have been dead a long time ago it she'd have been up against a *real* vamp.

That's his name, Alex. Not short for anything, he doesn't have a last name either. Just Alex.

"I thought I'd stop by and see what you complain about all the time." His detailed green eyes stared up to the school building behind me. Another thing, sunlight doesn't do zilch; in fact he can build up quite a nice tan.

"I don't complain." I sniffed. "I just point out the negatives."

"Geez and *I'm* supposed to be the pessimistic one." He looked back down at me, his brown hair falling slightly over his eyes.

"You do know that the trio of ogling girls back there are going to interrogate me for the rest of the day right?" I glared at him, standing in his jeans and white t-shirt, a blue shirt open over the top. That's right, no black in sight.

I saw his eyes glance round me and smile. I know my friends too well for their own good.

"You gonna tell them who I am?" He asked, looking back to my face again.

"Oh sure." I laughed, voice dripping with sarcasm. "They'd be so happy to hear that I'm friends with a Vampire. So happy they'll strap me into the white jacket and have me off to the padded room."

"Friends?" He repeated, looking a little more than put out. "That all?"

I hate it when he does this. Although I'd do anything for him it's hard to call him my "boyfriend". It's a complicated situation you must understand.

"Don't start this one." I glared. I often wonder why he chose me of all people. He's drop dead gorgeous and I'm, well I'm me. It doesn't quite add up in my mind, but maybe it's different inside a vampire brain. Then something does click inside my head. Oh clever, clever me. "Do you know what tonight is?"

"It's Halloween." He stated, placing his hands in his pockets.

"Ding ding first prize! Do you know what you win?"

"I'm afraid to ask."

"I have to take the brat trick or treating tonight, so my dad wants me to find someone to tag along." I told him, a rather dastardly smile forming on my face.

"Yeh, and?" Alex cocked his head, almost begging me to climb over the fence and kick him, hard.

"You're coming with me, since everyone else doesn't care enough." I answered smugly, placing both hands on my hips.

"What's in it for me?" He raised a skeptical eyebrow.

"The honor of knowing a girl and child aren't wandering around the streets at night, alone." I tapped my fingers upon the top of my arm. I knew he would do it, but the pleasure of teasing me first cannot be resisted. Too bad for him I'd learnt to answer back.

He sighed. "Sure."

I'd learnt well.

"So who is he?"

"What's his name?

"Where does he buy his clothes?"

I turned and stared at Ella like she'd just grown another beautiful blonde head.

"What? Bret needs some serious styling tips." She defended herself as I turned back to walking along the school hallway and into my own thoughts.

My friends continued firing obscene questions into my face as I glazed over. It wasn't like I could answer any of them truthfully.

"He's a vampire called Alex, and I think he goes to Barney's."

Please, my life is already complicated enough, I didn't need my friends thinking I needed psychiatric help; they probably do already. I really didn't expect to see him today. We usually have a routine where he'll come to my house and we'll either stay in my room or go somewhere. To the movies, pizza, the park, anywhere really. He calls it a date. I call it a social gathering. He'll always come to me, since I have no idea where he lives or what he actually does when I don't see him. I use that basis as to why we can't call this "meeting" a relationship. Heck he could have a job in the local grocery store and I wouldn't know! Though, I doubt that; I don't think I could see him in a place like that. He looks like he should work in one of those fancy men's fashion stores. Maybe I could ask a few more questions tonight whilst my bratling brother bothers little old ladies for candy. I'm pretty sure he'd tell me, he'd never been that secretive about his life before.

Hmmm, now that's an idea.

Instead of doing stupid Shakespeare, writing a little list of queries should keep my occupied for the next hour. That should drown out the insanely boring voice of my English teacher

Maybe this day was going to be better than I thought.

I hate Halloween. It's officially the worst holiday, ever. I decided that a very long time ago but now I have formally printed it into my skull. I sat and decided what candy I'd steal from my brother's pumpkin basket whilst he wasn't looking when the brat himself burst into the living room wearing his full Dracula attire. The fangs, the slicked back hair, the black almost suit-like outfit and matching black cape. He thinks he looks the bomb. I think he looks like a dweb.

"Ok you two, have fun!" My mother calls shrilly from the hallway, placing her cat ears straight upon her head with her whiskers tickling her face.

"I want you guys back by eight alright? No funny business." My dad set down the rules, though it's hard to take him seriously dressed as Captain Jack Sparrow. Johnny Depp shall never look sexy to me again.

"I got it already." I rolled my eyes, slumping up from the couch. "You can go now."

"Don't wait up!" Mother giggled as father whispered something into her *real* ear in what sounded like a cheesy pirate accent. My family could possibly scar me for life if I wasn't so docile.

"Come on Miya, the kids from school said they're gonna knock on old Blackman's house, he never gives out candy!" Jason pulled at my jeans. I frowned, agreeing with a nod and grabbing my coat as we approached the door.

"I guess he'll find us along the way."

As I opened the front door a set of emeralds glimmered back at me.

"Trick or treat?"

. . . .

You know what I hate more than Halloween? The cold. I walked along the sidewalk feeling like a living ice popsicle as Jason rushed up and down each driveway. He didn't have time to get cold; he was too busy running the ghoul marathon.

"Cold?"

I turned and glanced up at Alex. He was wearing a light black jacket but looked as though he was perfectly content about the weather. I thought Vampires had cold blood. That was when told me to stop comparing him to "some kind of reptile".

"No, I just like shivering. It's a hobby I picked up along with sneezing in peoples faces and not covering my mouth when I burp."

"Damn sarcasm." He mumbled, stopping and turning to face me as he took my hands in his, rubbing them between his palms to replace the lost heat. I glared up at him, thinking of ways to hurt the dweb when he'd finished returning the blood to my fingers.

"Guess what I got from Mrs. Swanskin?" Jason suddenly rushed up to me, shoving a large bar of pink candy into my face.

"Are you seriously planning to eat all that crap tonight?" I peered down into his overflowing basket, feeling slightly queasy.

"Don't spoil his fun." Alex scolded.

"*Yeah*, now I'm not letting you have any." Brother poked out his tongue before rushing ahead to the next door.

I would have given him a severe Chinese burn if my hands weren't already occupied.

I know right? You're probably wondering why Jason acted like his normal freaky self around Alex. He *kind* of knows who he is, from one past encounter I certainly won't be forgetting in a hurry. One night a few months back Alex's blood lust had called to me, which unsurprisingly is the norm for most of our encounters. In my state of hypovolemia I hadn't realised the door to my bedroom had been left wide open, so when my brother gawked in at the two of us it wasn't exactly explainable. We quickly separated when I saw him standing there, mouth agape and speechless for the first time in his young life.

"Does mum know you have a boyfriend?"

Those words were like music to my ears. I bribed him to keep quiet about my "boyfriend" if I gave him half my pocket money every week from then on. Our asses were saved, but my piggy bank has never felt so skinny. Apparently he'd failed to notice the long shiny fangs embedded into my throat, and **that** is how it shall stay.

"Why do you two gang up on me?" I whined, walking along to the next front whilst Jason already started slamming on the doorbell.

"You're too harsh on him." Alex replied, letting go of my newly toasty digits.

"Too harsh?" I spluttered. "You have *no* idea the torture he puts me through on daily basis."

"Yeh, but you love him." He grinned. I look away and grumbled before suddenly realising tonight's main task.

"Oh yeh!" I cried, fishing out the folded piece of paper from my coat pocket.

"What's that?"

"My Vampire questionnaire." I declared proudly. "Answer all questions right and you're a full blown vampire ready to take on the world, answer less than five correctly means you're a wimpy little bloodsucker who wouldn't say boo to his non-existent shadow."

"I've told you already we have shadows, and reflections." He sighed. "You watch too much TV."

"Question 1! How old are you; really?"

"Hmm, that's a tricky one." He placed a hand behind his head, looking deep in thought. "I'm 19."

"Seriously?" I turned to him, looking a little more than bemused.

"Well, in human years anyway." He shrugged, continuing along.

"So you are 133 in dog years." I complimented myself on my superhuman mathematical skills.

"Haha."

"Question 2, where the heck do you live?"

"Why do you care, and hold the phone; why are you asking these stupid questions?"

"What do you mean *why*?" I growled. "You seem to know everything about me and I know next to nothing about the guy who has a B positive smoothie every Friday night!"

"You mean your *boyfriend*?" He smirked, placing his hands in his pockets whilst leaning down slightly closer to my face.

"No, I don't." Screwing up my paper, I felt my temper flare. "I don't go for wimpy little bloodsuckers who won't say boo to their nonexistent shadow!"

Grabbing Jason's greedy little hand I began dragging him back to the house, ignoring his complaints of not visiting the other side of the street as I felt the blood rush to my cheeks.

Nothing was on TV. The usual scary movies that didn't even make Jason hide behind the couch bored me to death, though I did pick up some interesting ways to torture that ignorant parasite.

That cute, ignorant parasite.

I shook my head like a baby rattle, changing channel to distract my wondering thoughts. Peepers had his large face slobbering on my knee, acting like a drooling hot water bottle. Some channel about how to choose the right shade of white for your house showed up as the hundredth knock upon the front door disturbed me from my lazy night of cheesy commercials. Picking up the bowl of candy hidden upon the shelf from wandering little hands, I walked to door; passing the owner of the wondering little hands stuffing his face with crap up upon the kitchen stool. I opened the door with my most convincing "happy to see you" face, only for it to drop back into my usual scowl.

"Wow kid, that's some scary mask you've got on." I shoved the bowl at him. "Here, choke on it."

"Miya." Alex grumbled, calling after me as I stalked back to my happy hideaway.

Heaving myself back onto the couch Peepers opened his eyes and gave me a grunt as a complaint of being disturbed, but seeing the bundle of messy brown hair heading my way had him jumping onto the floor, growling like a possessed demon.

"I hope you didn't leave the bowl in the kitchen." I said spoke, throwing small pieces of popcorn into my mouth.

"Call the devil hound away and I might just tell you."

"Peepers, go sit with confectionary child." I told my Great Dane. It's only to be expected that most find Peepers a little scary, he's taller than my dad when he's on his hind legs. The canine dropped his ears and trotted out into the hallway.

"I didn't mean to hurt your feelings earlier." I heard Alex's voice from the middle of the room; a little behind me so he was cleverly out of my sight.

"It just means you're not a real vampire." I replied, crossing my arms over my chest with a smug look upon my face. "*Real* bloodsucking demons aren't get scared of little doggies."

"Little?" He choked. I smirked, happy with my succession of making Mr. Cool slip up on his oh so convincing muted exterior.

"I hate it when you're mad at me." His voice suddenly whispered into my ear, making me jump halfway across the couch. Stupid vampires with their stupid super silent feet. His arms wrapped around my front, resting his chin on my right shoulder as I continued to ignore his affections.

"Concentrate on the man painting the wall, concentrate!" I felt his breath on my neck, making my skin tingle.

"I'm sorry ok? Now please stop with the silent treatment, it doesn't suit you."

"What's that supposed to mean?" I turned and glared at him.

"That's better." He smiled, leaning his arms on the back of the couch as I knelt upon the cushions, sighing. I was never really good at winning these sorts of arguments. Not with that smile anyways.

. . . .

"So let me get this straight, he's painting the whole room white?"

"No, he's using that as an undercoat before he paints it Burgundy."

"I'll never understand these makeover shows, they're so complicated."

I smiled to myself; our eyes staying glued to the screen. I fitted perfectly between his arm and the back of the couch, my head moving up and down against his breathing with Alex himself propped up against the furniture arm. It always seemed to soothe me to hear his breathing, mostly to make sure he's actually a living being and not a figment of my over active imagination. My head lolled upon his chest, toes curling inside my pig patterned socks.

Present from Sophie from her trip to Los Angeles. She goes to the city of angels; and brings me back pig socks.

"You just have a simple mind." I replied.

Alex looked down at me whilst I stared straight back. "It must be to put up with you."

I smiled, snuggling up further into his warm body as I closed my eyes. "You love me really."

"You don't know how much."

My eyes sparked right back open. Did he want to run that past me again? Just as I went to open my mouth a large heaving sound echoed out from the kitchen, a small yelp accompanying it. Peepers ran back into the room, covered in something I'd rather not explain.

"Miya, I think I ate too much."

The meek groan came from the doorway where Jason stood, his eaten Halloween candy saying a rather rancid hello down his stench soaked front.

I let out a rather large yawn whilst trekking back down the stairs. After removing my brothers foul smelling clothing and dunking him into the bath the rather quiet little bratling had dozed off as I put him to bed. He's always so eerily silent after he's unwell; I think he'd learnt his lesson. As I reached the last step Peepers came bounding in from the back door connected to the kitchen, dripping wet. Of course he thought the opportune moment to shake himself dry would be right in front of yours truly.

"You're welcome!" I screeched; the smell of wet dog sinking into my t-shirt as the dozy canine trotted away. It was then that Alex chose the perfect moment to make his appearance, cropping up as my temper started to flare.

"You know this thing called a towel?" I stared at him. "Use it!"

"Hey it was hard enough getting him to let me hose him down, he ran off before I could even get one!" He defended.

"Well, at least he doesn't stink anymore." I grumbled. "No more than he usually does anyway."

"So, was your Halloween eventful?" He asked, leaning against the hallway wall.

"It's *still* Halloween." I answered, looking confused. Alex shook his brunette head, pointing up to the clock inside the living room. The hands read 5 minutes to midnight.

"Only for another few minutes." He spoke.

I slumped my shoulders, letting out an exasperated sigh.

"At least I don't have to wait much longer for this damn holiday to be over."

Before I could even begin to object Alex took my hand in his, pulling me into the living room. Walking into the middle of the scope he then turned and faced me.

"What?" I looked up, slightly wary. "You're not gonna turn into a vampire bat or something are you?"

"Shut up, and dance with me." He extended his hands to me.

"I think I'd rather see you turn into a bat."

"Do you think that mouth of yours could take a rest for a while?" He asked, wrapping his arm around my middle, pulling me closer. "Let your feet do the talking."

Flashing Lights

I was too tired to continue arguing as I felt his free hand link fingers with mine.

"There's no music."

"You don't need music."

Once again my head rested against his front, his heartbeat echoing inside my head. As my eyes closed as we started to move from side to side, my other hand snaking its way around his neck.

His head rested near to the top of mine as I felt the hot air from his lungs blow out onto my hair. His hands were warm like always, and as he brought our linked digits upwards from the side towards his face I felt myself blush. He kissed the back of my hand. His lips were so soft against my skin, I ached to fall asleep and never wake up as the musical chimes from my father's Swedish clock brought us into a new morning.

Chapter 3

"Miya!"

My eyes darted open, suddenly feeling a huge lump on top of me. Oh wonderful.

"What?" I groused; looking up to my brother's happy little face.

"Mum and dad are taking me to the zoo today and because you were so nice to me last night, I'm gonna buy you a present!"

My heart swelled up as I heard Jason's sweet brotherly love, but it didn't last long.

"Wonderful, now get out of my room." I turned onto my side, the thump of his backside hitting my floor a rather pleasing sound.

"I can't get mad at you today sis, see ya later!" He grinned and stood up, racing out of my room whilst leaving the door ajar.

Saturdays.

I have three choices of what to do with my life on a Saturday.

Option one: call up my friends and prance about town.

Option two: to go with my folks to wherever the bratling wants to go on a Saturday.

Option three: well, sleeping in.

I would love to have Option three as my designated chore, but my mother insists that I arise from my hollow and do something productive with my day. I'm surprised she and dad aren't hung-over with their heads down the toilet, but I suppose experience comes with age. That's why she makes sure everyone knows to leave my bedroom door open before they leave, to make sure I "broaden my horizons". Peepers will always get bored and sulk up here, looking for attention. It's pretty hard to ignore him as even if you do drop back off; his fat behind trying to curl up on top of you sure is a hell of a wakeup call. So I always manage to get up, make myself some breakfast and tune into some cartoons, feeding Peepers the scraps from my toast. I would normally have the house to myself, but someone else seems to have figured out that my day is free.

He must have put me to bed when I dozed off last night. I felt my neck… and sighed.

He didn't feed.

It hadn't been a week yet since he last did it, but I always thought the temptation would be too much for him, especially if I'm unconscious. It makes me feel quite loved, knowing that he doesn't take advantage. Pulling on a jumper over my pyjamas I stood and wondered if he was going to show up today. At least he left through the correct entrance this time, glancing at my closed window.

The usual occurs; I sat on the couch with a blanket over my crossed legs. It's pretty cold outside and I needed all the warmth I could get. Luckily Peepers was on hand to slob over my lap whilst I leant my plate on top of his large back. I made a mental note that this dog needs to cut down on the treats.

I'm always cold, you must have realised that now. It's because of me being so ill as kid. I'm still having regular checkups and the odd injection every now and then, but it was far worse years ago. I have a very weak immune system, which means any little germ that goes around, I got. I hardly remember going to school, I was always off hidden away in my bedroom or in the hell they call hospital. The worst thing was I couldn't see any of my friends and hardly any of my family since they could have possibly infected me. I didn't see Peepers for a very long time, in fact I wasn't allowed to go anywhere near him. He was only a puppy then but he was still a gentle giant. I like to think of our Saturday routines as make up for the amount of time we lost when were we both younger. That's probably why this dog is so spoilt.

Powerpuff Girls blared onto my screen as a series of frantic rasps descended upon the front door. It's pretty hard to shove a 10 stone dog from your frame, but after many tries I succeeded and padded towards the door, which from the sound of might have split in half.

"I'm coming already!" I yelled; ready to give the owner a piece of my mind. I could barely give a breath before someone shoved me back onto the wall adjacent to the open entry. I hissed slightly from the pain scaling up my back before I stared into the owners eyes. There was wide and very much alive, moving along my face with fear inside the baby blue colour of them.

"Where is it?" He asked, looking as petrified as I was.

"What are you talking about?" I cried, trying to push his rather chubby hands away from my shoulders.

"You know!" He kept repeating, shoving me back against the wall. Another wave of pain coursed through my body and sleep seemed so very wondrous. Sudden low growls made the boy snap back, setting my shoulders loose. He stared down at Peepers standing by the front room doorway, baring his teeth as he continued to growl like some kind of wild animal. I can't remember the last time Peepers growled like that, but I certainly wasn't complaining. The boy stood there for a moment as I tried to catch my stolen breath, staring down at my dog with an unexplainable emotion stretched along his face. He was quite plump in frame, though only a few centimetres taller than me. Sweat glistened off his forehead and through his spiky black hair. Nothing registered inside me for a few moments, my mind was blank. Who the heck was he? What could I have that he seemed to be after? My thoughts shot back down to earth as his neck cracked, eyes glanced up towards the stairs. Within a blink of an eye he'd sprang through the air, thudding onto the upstairs landing. My heart skipped a beat as he ran down towards my room.

Vampire.

Peepers turned, barking wildly as he bounded up the stairs after him.

"Wait!" I heard myself cry, chasing after the duo.

The sound of glass breaking and objects being thrown to the floor made me shake as I approached the door. The boy was holding the red smoky ball in his hands tightly, backed into a corner by Peepers as my room sat in a state of chaos.

"What are you doing?" I shrieked, running behind Peepers.

"This isn't yours!" The boy yelled at me over Peeper's growls. "It doesn't belong to you!"

"I know what you are." I stared into his face whilst trying to show no fear, though my legs were ready to turn into mush.

The boy didn't react; instead he closed his eyes tight and tried to run past the two of us at lightning speed. It was then the chilling sound of something heavy hitting the wall made me jump back in fright. Alex stood just inside of my room with his hand around the foreigner's neck, feet dangling. His eyes stared through the soul of the stranger, the green looking almost… evil.

"The door was open."

Chapter 4

"He's a vampire."

"I know."

My legs couldn't take no more. My body slumped to the floor, half in relief and half in exhaustion. I heard a loud thump as the boy was dropped to the floor a few inches in front of me with just Alex's legs separating us. He snatched back the red ball from the boy's sweaty hands and placed it delicately back on my desk, amidst the massacre of papers and books.

"I thought you'd have known better than this." He spoke calmly, his tone harder and much more frightening than the usual cocky tenor I'm used to hearing. Then it clicks.

"You know him?" I cried, the spluttering of hoarse coughs following suit.

"I wish I didn't."

"I'm sorry!" The boy started to warble, groveling down at Alex's feet. "I didn't mean to do any harm!"

"You always were such a sniveling tick." Alex replied, turning away and bending down to face me.

"Who is he?" I asked, trying to rid the pain that echoed through my lungs.

"Someone who gives our kind a bad name." His eyes looked into mine, helping me to my feet. I felt Peepers' head brush under my hand as I took deep breaths, glancing down at the mess of demon sniveling on my wooden floor.

"He's an idiot." Alex replied, looking down at the mysterious vampire. "But he didn't mean to hurt you; he couldn't even if he tried."

I looked up at Alex in confusion. I was going to have a severely monstrous headache later on.

"It's true, I just couldn't believe that he'd give it to someone he's barely known for five minutes." He sniffed. "My primal instincts took over."

Scratch that, the headache had hit me like a ten ton weight.

"Give me what? The ball?" I asked. "It's just a glass paperweight."

"Exactly." Alex repeated down to him. "A glass paperweight."

I was sure his tone was slightly odd.

Ok, I'd gathered the fact that this guy's name was Ron, but still nothing seed to be adding up.

"Ron is an accident prone moron, but he means well." Alex rolled his eyes.

"I sincerely apologize." The boy seemed to cheer up immediately, standing and brushing down his baggy clothes. "Like I said, it's primal instincts. Plus, I've always wanted to see Alex's soul."

I groaned, holding my head. " I need to sit down."

"How did you know I was a vampire?"

"Maybe it was the fact that you jumped fifty feet into the air?"

"Really, do you think it was that far?"

I slumped back onto the side of my bed, groaning.

"Here." Alex stood over me, a glass of water and a few aspirin in his hand. I took both, shoving the pills into my throat like my life depended on it. I had a feeling my confusion would only get worse as the conversation continued, better stock up now.

"I didn't tell you about Ron before because I didn't think it was important, and I didn't think he would barge into your house." Alex glared down at the vampire in question, a nervous laugh emitting from such vampires mouth.

"So let me get this straight, you darted into my room all for the sake of a *paperweight?*"

"I'm like a magpie, I love shiny things." He chuckled. I narrowed my eyes. Something in his voice didn't convince me.

"Ok fine." I didn't bother to interrogate, for that is what Alex would be subjected to later on. "But what is this soul business you're talking about?"

"The human soul is said to leave the body when it dies, and wanders through the afterlife for all eternity." Ron explained, his legs crossed looking like a Buddha. "A vampire doesn't have a soul like you do, and so some seek out one to share."

I looked up to Alex, sitting beside me on top of my duvet.

"You're sharing my soul?"

"I thank you for being so kind." He smiled.

"You could have asked." I grumbled, turning back to Ron.

"It's a good thing! You're Alex's soul." Ron beamed before looking deep in thought. "Though to be honest, you seem a pretty funny choice."

I raised an eyebrow. "Just what is meant by that?"

"Well normally strong vampires go for strong humans." He replied.

"I *am* strong!"

"He means in health terms." Alex told me. "You're health is weak compared to other humans."

"Then why did you pick me?" I asked, genuinely concerned.

"Do you really need an answer for that?" He smiled softly. My cheeks flushed.

"Gees, I didn't know you liked this girl so much." Ron scratched the back of his head. "I just thought she was another one of your stages."

The headache didn't seem to be going away anytime soon.

"Stages?" I repeated, glaring up at Alex. I could tell he was quite scared, judging from the way he placed his hands up in front of himself like a defenseless kid. "So, how many "souls" have you shared?"

"Oh, Vampires like to experiment." Ron said casually, not noticing the world of pain Alex was surely promising him through deathly green eyes. "They usually go with a few before finding their true soul."

"Well." I stand up. "See if I ever share my soul with you again!"

"But you're his true soul!" Ron tried to grab my attention. "Otherwise he wouldn't have given you the "paperweight"."

I glanced down at Ron, feeling only slightly better.

"That's why I was so uptight about him giving it to you so early; I thought he might have been making a mistake."

"Well I'll use that paperweight as a weapon for murder if you two bloodsucking idiots don't start cleaning my room!" I snapped, slamming my bedroom door behind me. Please! Enough of hocus pocus for a while; I want sanity for once on my life!

No such luck.

"What are you doing?"

"I'm cleaning."

"No, you're wearing a hole into the marble."

I growled and threw the cloth onto the table, walking towards the sink.

"I'll wear a hole into your head if you don't fly back up those stairs." I warned him, running the hot water.

"Ron has a big mouth."

"By the sounds of it you have a big selection of souls in your cabinet." I snapped, squeezing in the washing liquid.

"No, I don't." Alex replied firmly. "Everyone has a few relationships before they settle down, why should a vampire be any different?"

I didn't answer, shoving a dirty plate into the warm foam.

"You're jealous, aren't you?"

"NO!" I screeched for the entire street to hear as I turned to face him. "I JUST DON'T LIKE FEELING USED!"

His gaze softened and I felt a few tears drips down my cheeks. I shut my eyes tight, turning back around and mentally cursing myself for letting my guard down so easily. Another set of hands suddenly started to run down my arms, dropping down into the water to join my own.

"I've never seen you cry." Alex's soft voice whispered to me, his chest vibrating onto my back.

"No one has, well apart from my family." I replied, my voice slightly calmer. "I've learnt that crying gets you nowhere."

"Then why are you crying now?"

The silence after he spoke nerve shattering. It made me want to become a five year old again, hiding myself under the kitchen table with hands over my ears and eyes firmly shut until the monsters went away.

"Well, you have a funny effect on me." I joked, feeling his hands on top of mine under the frothy fluid.

"That's funny, because you have a funny effect on me too." He replied, his lips closer to my ear. "That's why you have my paperweight."

I turned around slowly whilst his hands still remained in the soapy mixture, one eyebrow raised as I crossed my arms over.

"Other girls get flowers and chocolates, I get a paperweight."

"A very *pretty* paperweight."

I couldn't help but laugh as he grinned down at me. My eyes lock onto his, and that butterfly feeling people get in those soppy romantic movies hit me quick. Why does he have this effect on me?

"For a very pretty soul." He smiled, bending his arms so his face came closer to mine. This time I didn't object as our foreheads touched, feeling his lips gently graze my own. His green eyes widened slightly when I placed two fingers on his wandering mouth.

"Primal instincts?" I asked.

"Vampires are descended from primitive animals." He explained. "Fight or flight, kill or protect. We're very territorial."

My face must have scrunched up, because he gave me a funny look.

"What?"

"You're going to pee on me, aren't you?"

. . . .

I sat and watched Ron, his tongue out of the side of his mouth, fingers dancing along the game controller whilst staring at the TV. Peepers was slumped in the corner on his side, a lot calmer knowing Ron wasn't going to try and kill me.

"We go way back." Alex spoke as we sat upon my bed, my newly cleaned room pristine once again. "He stuck to me like glue."

"He obviously cares a lot about you." I smiled, watching the boy curse the game hero for deciding to die a bloody death.

"He acts before thinks." Alex studied his fellow Vampire. "Which makes him a numbskull."

"A *caring* numbskull." I nudged him gently. "Does he live with you?"

"Ron likes to do his own thing, like me." He responded. "I only see him when he wants something."

"Does he have a soul?"

"*Please*, he's about as good with women as he is that game."

"He seems happy enough." I looked down back at the aloof demon. "He seems to care more about *your* soul."

"I'm guessing for a very good reason." Alex yawned, stretching his arms.

I cocked my head, curious. "And that would be?"

"Slayers of course."

Chapter 5

Slayer.

The word unnerves me a little. After everything Alex told me about the dumb stories surrounding Vampires, I thought Slayers would have been the most ridiculous. Apparently I was wrong.

"They're real alright." Ron shivered, munching down on a pizza slice. "They scare the ever-loving crap outta me."

I ignored the waterfall of crumbs erupting from his mouth. Sitting inside the pizza place a few blocks down from where I live, I was listening to every single word spoken. I had to get out of that house, I was slowly going insane.

"You mean actual human beings know about you?" I enquired.

"Know about us? They want to *kill* us." Alex replied, sitting beside me.

"How? Like with stakes, swords dipped in silver, large crosses?"

"You *do* watch too much TV." Alex cocked his head.

"Same way you kill humans, but more advanced. Since we're so fast and agile it's hard to get a good target, but these Slayers can be *just* as fast and *just* as cunning." Ron added, picking up another piece. I barely nibbled at my own pepperoni surprise.

"You mean, like a hunt?" I asked, bringing my coke straw to my mouth.

"Now you know how those poor little foxes feel."

Alex picked up his cream soda. "Have you ever heard of a Sang Rose?"

"Yeh." I replied, thinking back to my collection of Japanese Manga. I get a lot of inspiration from the beautiful pictures for my own artwork. Who says I'm not cultured? "It's a gun used to kill vampires."

Alex kept looking at me, right up until I felt my tongue hit the carpet.

"You're kidding right?"

"Evil little things they are." Ron shivered, slurping more of his own soda. "They always get ya first time."

"Ok ok." I exhaled, trying to fix the jigsaw together inside my head. "So you mean to say there are people out there now, carrying vampire killing guns and shooting at anything with unusually long front teeth?"

"They're not people." Alex spoke, his voice serious and firm. "They're murderers."

"There's one particular group that has our kind wetting our pants." Ron wiped his mouth and hands. "They're called the Angels of God."

The name sent chills down my spine, suddenly losing what was left of my appetite all together.

"I don't know much about them, but I'm sure Alex could tell you a thing or two." Ron's blue irises looked from me to Alex before quickly setting back to me again. I turned to him almost immediately, my curiosity going into overload.

"Not here." He whispered, his green eyes a mere dull to what I was used to.

I was pretty sure I wasn't going to be rid of those two so easily, but after cleverly remembering Peepers needed a walk, Ron quickly dismissed himself.

Since Peepers is such a large canine the local doggie park isn't big enough for him to roam around in. He's also quite clumsy, little old dears taking their Chihuahuas for a scuttle would be too easy a target. This is why our family always takes him over the large field a few blocks away from the house. You can see the entire city from the top of the large hill and it's quite a comforting sight. Throwing the large rubber toy in the direction of the sloping mount, I watched Peepers gallop after it as Alex stood beside me, the wind blowing through his shirt.

"My parents were killed by Slayers, the ones Ron told you about." He suddenly spoke.

I dug my nails into Peepers leash.

"How did you escape?"

"My mother." His voice quieted, eyes gazing out across the impending sunset. "She told me to run, run and don't stop. Run and don't look back. They nearly caught me, but I was lucky."

"You've never talked about your parents before." I replied, pushing a stray hair behind my ear.

"It's the past, where it needs to stay." He told me, hands in his jean pockets.

"You've never tried to find them, get them back for what they did?" I glanced up to him face. It's unsure what goes around in that head of his, I can never tell.

"Two wrongs don't make a right Miya." He responded after a few short moments. "They have families too."

I looked down at the grass beneath my shadow, a sudden feeling of guilt running through my spine.

"That's what they are, one big family."

I looked back up, pulling a muscle in my neck. I ignored the pain.

"One big family?"

"Fathers, mothers, daughters, sons, nieces, nephews, cousins, I could go on." He answered; his hair flying slightly to the side of his head. "They all learn the ways of a slayer from the moment they're born, and become killing machines before they even leave school. It's those eyes, those grey eyes that frighten us the most."

I felt another shiver find its way down my back, burying my face into the warm material of my scarf.

"There's hundreds of them, all spread out across the globe, trying to wipe out the Vampire race completely." His eyes narrowed across the afternoon sunset. "There's a war going on, and no one else can see it."

"How long has it been going on like this?" I asked as Peeper's walks back up to me, toy proudly clamped between his jaws. After a few minutes of playing tug of war I threw it back towards the grass, the canine almost flying down the hill to catch it.

"Ah, hundreds of years, and I have a feeling it'll carry on for much longer."

My face contorted. "Why? Why would they want to do this? You aren't killing everyone in sight; you're living peacefully alongside us."

"We are devils." Alex didn't stir. "They are Angels, sent to this earth to rid the world of evil. They won't stop until their will has been accomplished."

"Then they'll come for you, won't they?"

He snapped back into reality and glanced down. "Perhaps, but they won't kill me." He smiled, sounding with a ring of familiar cockiness. Oh what a surprise. "I'm too good for that."

"You know sometimes I wonder what's bigger; my dog or your ego." I raised an eyebrow.

"Or my heart?"

"Do you have one?"

"You have my heart."

"That's so cheesy, and who says I want it?" I placed my gloved hands onto my hips.

"You do." Alex replied. "If you didn't, you would have told me so."

I sniffed. "I'm not *that* frank."

"Well..." Alex walked down the other side of the hill, a smirk appearing on the side of his face.

"Don't you dare walk away!" I chased after him, hearing Peeper's loud panting coming up behind me. "Answer me!"

My Sunday flies by like usual. Homework and chores took up most of my precious free time, leaving me too exhausted to do anything else by the end of it all. My life would be duller than the colour of Grandma's house if it wasn't for Alex. It would be normal too.

"So how was your family dinner?" I asked Sophie whilst rummaging through my school locker Monday morning. It's like Aladdin's cave and along with Mimi; Magpie is also another wonderful nickname the girls have given me. Such good friends.

"How do you think it went?" Sophie grumbled, leaning against the metal spaces beside my open one, frowning. "Their grandmother always criticizes me for *something*."

"What was it this time?"

"My hair."

I turned and stared at Sophie in utter amazement. I've always been envious of her shiny, thick black hair. It's never out of place and looks good no matter how she does it. Unlike mine, this seems to want to mould into the shape of wild hay.

"You're kidding right?"

"She said girls should have long silky hair, like her precious dumplings." Sophie stuck out her tongue is distaste. Her eyes narrowed and her olive skin wrinkled but she still looks good. Damn her.

"The tweevil's have hair like a Barbie doll." I snorted, turning back my concentration to the bomb site that is my cave of a thousand wonders. It's true. Their long brown hair is only long because the amount of *fake* hair stitched in. Emily wanted to hold a petition against the amount of hair extensions used around the world. She said people in poverty stricken countries shave their head just so other people can look good. I was fully ready to sign, but our Principal decided against the idea. Funnily enough it was after an appointment at the Salon.

"Though my dad did stick up for me, he's always loved my hair." Sophie sighed happily, clutching her books against her lap.

"Him and the rest of the population." I smiled, finding my lost English book and shutting my locker.

"Heads up!"

I barely had time to react before a large brown football came hurtling down the hallway in my direction. I closed my eyes and hoped it wouldn't hurt too much. I live down embarrassment pretty easily, so I didn't care about that side of this blink of an eye occurrence. Strange enough though, it seemed to be taking its sweet time.

The sound of awes and wows entered my ears. I dared to open one eye, then the other. A hand held the ball inches away from my face, suddenly holding it up to the air and throwing it back down the school corridor.

"You should watch out." The male voice turned to my direction as I blinked up to the owner. He was tall and quite slim; his blonde hair was short against his almost white skin. Then I saw them, and I was sure my heart stopped for just one terrifying moment. "You don't know who might sneak up on you."

He walked away back down the busy corridor, the rest of the school body already moving on.

"Damn he's got quick reflexes!" Sophie stood beside me, watching the boy leave. "Did you see how fast he caught that ball?"

I didn't answer. My body felt stuck to the floor as I replayed that face again and again inside my head. Those eyes. Those grey eyes.

Chapter 6

My head was swimming for the rest of the day, I couldn't concentrate on anything. Those eyes were fermented inside of my head and they wouldn't leave me alone. Could he really be a slayer, or was I just overreacting? I mean come on; he goes to this school! How could I have not seen him around before? Maybe I *did* see him before, but I just didn't take any notice? Whatever it is, it's driving me to the point of insanity.

I need to tell Alex. Problem is I don't know where he is, and I wouldn't have a clue where to start looking for him. He hardly ever visits me during the week. He says studies come before dates. I do tend to remind him that we don't have "dates"; just social gatherings. He seems to think I'm joking.

When the school bell rings for the final time that day I felt a huge sigh of relief wash over me as I scrambled out of my seat and through the door like a rocket. I prayed I wouldn't see that boy again; I just wanted to get out of this place and back home. I also prayed that Alex will have the sense to come see me that night. Hopefully he'd sense the urgency coming from me, everyone else probably can.

Hmmm, maybe I'll send out a bat signal.

Get it? Ok I'll stop.

My dad doesn't finish work until late so I always end up walking home, except if Ella's mum gives us a lift. I found out she wasn't, since Ella decided to be ill and not come in today. Pfft, and they call *me* the sickly child! That girl is sick more times than Peepers were when he drunk that bucket full of bleach. Just don't ask.

I wrapped my coat tighter around my body as I said my goodbyes to the others, walking quickly down the street. My hands and feet were numb and I just wanted to get home. This day has been too much.

Of course when I felt a hand place itself upon my shoulder I yelled and jumped away in unspeakable fright.

"Hey!" Came the annoyed voice, rubbing his ears. "Careful with the sensitive hearing would ya?"

Right at that moment I want to kick Ron for being so idiotic, but I decided to hold back. I could have hugged him for not being the Grey eyed boy too. I decided to hold back on that as well.

"Didn't anyone teach you not to sneak up on people like that?" I hissed, clutching my bag closer to my front in case he could see my heart thumping out of my chest.

"Sorry." He replied through mumbles of doughnut batter. I could smell the sugary delights excreting from the bag he held in his other hand and it made my stomach wail for nutrition. "What's got you in such a jumpy mood anyways?"

"I'll tell you if you share that bag with me." I answered, eying it down like a predator stalking its prey.

I'm not entirely sure if it's because he's eaten too many doughnuts or what I had just told him, but Ron had turned a sickly white. I watched his frozen face as I gobbled down my third doughnut, satisfying my wild gut. It's then I realised I didn't have lunch today. Now that's very unlike me. God how bad can even a glimpse of these Slayers affect you?

"Are you sure they were grey?"

"I don't forget eyes like that so easily." I replied, licking the sugar from my fingers as we shared the stone wall that encased a water feature inside the park. Any colder and I'm sure it would have turned into an ice rink.

Again Ron didn't talk and seemed to be in a state of thought. I've never seen Ron actually thinking before, it unnerved me a little.

"Well, do you think it's one of them?" I asked after a little while longer of unbearable silence.

"I couldn't tell ya." He finally spoke, a long breath exhaling from his lungs. "I've never actually seen one before."

"Then I guess Alex would be the only one to know." I looked at him, bringing my legs to my chin.

"If they are, he'll know."

"What will he do?" I asked, glancing down into the freezing water, ripples destroyed against the stone.

"We'll probably hit the road." Ron replied casually. "No sense in hanging around here if they know where to find us."

The fact that he said the words so casually cut even deeper into my already splintered soul.

I couldn't do my essay on the fungi of South America. I couldn't help mother cook dinner. I could barely listen to Jason explain the different levels of his video game; instead I just stared idly at the wall.

I couldn't stomach my linguini pasta and mum's decided to put Peepers on the Atkins, no carbs for him. That means she'd still see my plate still full.

"Not hungry?" She asked, sitting adjacent to me at the kitchen table.

Dang it.

"Not really." I replied. I knew what was coming.

"Hmmm." She placed her hand over my forehead. "You do feel a little warm."

"Does that mean Miya's not going to school tomorrow?" Jason came up for air; pasta sauce around his chubby little face. "Because if she is I don't wanna go either."

"Whether or not Miya goes in, you're going in." My mother told him sternly before directing her attention back to me. "Why don't you go to bed honey, see how you feel in morning?"

I know how I'd feel in the morning. Exactly the same as I felt now, but probably ten times worse. I'm not an early bird.

I didn't tell her this, she didn't know what was going on in my head right then and she'd probably book me a doctor's appointment if she did. The trek up the stairs felt twice as long as it usually did, my whole body aches.

Screw bed, I'd take a bath. They always seemed to relax me, plus the door blocks out the sound of my family. I know, I'm unsociable, and I could care less.

I felt like a load has been lifted off my shoulders as I sank into the warm water. Letting the bubble bath work its magic I leant back on my mother's bath pillow and closed my eyes, trying to figure that fickle thing known as my life. It makes my head hurt.

"Why do girls like bubble baths so much?"

I nearly fell under at the sound of the voice coming from the bathroom window. I covered my whole body under the froth and glance upwards to see Alex sitting at the windowsill. I would have screamed bloody murder if I didn't know his voice as well as I did.

"Catch you at a bad time?" He grinned. I replied with a stream of bubbles from my half drowned mouth.

"Come on, it's not like it's something I've never seen before."

Gripping onto the nearest thing I could get hold of I threw it right at his smug looking face, but instead hitting his arm and knocking him out of the building. What the hell did I throw?

"Nice to see you too." His voice came back into earshot, hovering back to his place at the window frame. Don't ask me how he does that.

"Perv." I grumbled, sitting up a little further and still feeling desperately self-conscious. "You've never seen me naked."

"I'd like to."

I searched around for another bathroom missile. "I always knew you were one of those guys." I glared. "A peeping tom who likes to watch girls naked."

"Nope, only you."

"Hah, good luck with that one." I scoffed.

"Ron said you had something to talk to me about." Alex rested his arms on his bent knees. The window is a little small for a guy like him, and I had to hold back a giggle. The matter at hand suddenly came swimming back.

"Are you going to leave?"

"You saw one, which means more probably aren't that far away." He replied. "They probably already know about me and Ron."

"You didn't answer my question."

"I think you know the answer."

"Well I think that you think that I know." My face screwed up with concentration. "But I also think that you know that I think that you know."

"English please?"

"I don't think you will."

"As you like to say; ding ding first prize, wanna know what you win?"

I smile, glancing down at the water.

"You win the knowledge that I'm not going anywhere."

"Nyeh."

"What?"

"That all?"

"You can see me naked if you like, though I'll have to see you first. Make it an even trade."

I splashed at him with my foot.

"I'll take my prize and leave, thank you very much."

Alex chuckled, leaning back in his tiny hollow.

"It'll happen eventually."

"Not in my lifetime."

"Prude."

"Perv."

I caught Alex glancing at the red paperweight yet again as I blow dried my hair. Of course it doesn't go straight even when I try my hardest, so I settled for kinks and give up.

"You look at that thing like your life depended on it." I sagged onto my bed, watching him roll from side to side on my computer chair.

He gave a simple smile, taking his eyes from the ball and slowly rolling them towards me. It always gives me butterflies when he does that. God he's perfect. Maybe he's a secret model? I won't choke on my doughnuts if I happen to see him up on a billboard someday. I keep thinking to ask Ron where he got those delicious little bites.

"I like your hair like that."

I stared back at him like he'd just been released early from the happy farm.

"You are kidding right?" I shook my messy mane, blowing a piece away from my face. "It's like a five year old kid's doodle."

"Will you please for once in your life stop putting yourself down?" He shook his own head of sleek brown hair, standing up and walking towards me. If he was a girl I would have plaited it by now. "I love your hair, I love your eyes, and I love your mouth."

"You're starting to sound like one of those guys from my mum's soap operas." I raise a skeptical eyebrow, crossing my arms over my middle as he rested his knees on top of my duvet, looking over me.

"And you can't take a compliment." He replies, settling his behind on his heels.

I study him for a bit longer. He looks quite pale, and I wonder something.

"You're hungry, aren't you?"

Obviously my outburst startled him, as his green eyes widened and looked away at my window.

"I'm fine."

"Yeh, right." I replied, knowing him all too well. I moved onto my knees and shuffled closer. "Here."

I moved my hair from one side of my face, leaving my neck bare in front of him.

"I can't." He answered stubbornly whilst still concentrating on the window, his fingers digging into his jeans.

"Why, because you've already done it this week?" I rolled my eyes. "Hello, you're supposed to be feeding every day anyways. Stop being such a chicken and do it already."

I know what you're thinking. I'm mad, letting a vampire willingly suck my blood. It doesn't hurt, it just feels like when you have a blood test, but obviously the needle is him and I don't get a drink and a biscuit afterwards. I know he won't take more than what I can handle, I trust him. The only thing that bugs me is why he doesn't seem to trust himself.

"Alex." I whisper, bringing my hand to his cheek. It's so smooth and warm, much like when his eyes look into mine. As expected he does just that, and the softness that gradually overcomes them means I have to close my eyes.

I don't want to see them turn red; I don't want to his see his fangs either. The last thing I see before I let in the darkness is the paperweight on my desk. The red smoke ball; the clouds moving around gracefully as he lowered his head to my shoulder.

Chapter 7

I woke up the next morning as I usually did after those nights; freezing.

"Shut the damn window after you go!" I cried out to no one, kicking the covers from my body and stomping over to the source of my Icelandic room. If he wasn't so fast I'd kick his ass from here back to Transylvania.

For today's fashion fix I decided on a denim skirt and long grey t-shirt. Don't worry I'm not completely out of my mind. Nice thick woolly grey tights would keep those sticks called legs warm for the day, accompanied with long, flat brown boots. Of course I wrap my brown scarf around my neck as I head down the stairs at the smell of burning toast. Now this scarf is for two reasons. The first one is obvious. It's still freezing outside and with my crappy susceptible internal organs I'll catch a cold before I set foot out the door. The other reason is because everyone at school will gawk at the large red patch on my neck.

A hickey? Please. After Alex bites me I get a funny little rash come up with the two tiny fang marks, and it's not exactly pretty. Luckily for me it goes down after a while, so I don't wear this thing for days in a row. Then everyone will *definitely* think I have a love bite. I smile to myself. In way, I guess it is. Not that I'd ever tell him that.

"Did you see The O.C last night?"

"My family doesn't like teenage soap operas. They say they're too sexually strung."

"Does your family watch *anything* Emily?"

"Well, the channel of peace and well fortune is often on when I get back."

"How thrilling."

For once the chatter didn't fly over my head like usual, and I smiled as my friends whispered amongst themselves inside the classroom. I tried getting down as many science equations being written up on the whiteboard as I could, whilst at the same time trying to understand the latest dramas in Ella's TV viewing; very bad TV viewing. I sighed softly to myself as I leant upon the window. My eyes soon spotted another class jumping around out on the football field. I didn't envy them, it was freezing outside and the girls had to wear shorts according to the stupid school procedure. Well the boys look more tortured than the ladies did as I watched the gaggle spluttering around the field whilst the teacher blew on his whistle like his life depended on it. Cross country running, ah what a pain. I stifled a laugh as most of the poor boys struggled around after a few laps, but carried on in hope the girls will notice their achievement. Alex can run so ridiculously fast it makes my head spin. He once asked me if I wanted to run with him one time. Only if he wanted my delicious lunch of Mexican chili and tacos down his front was my blunt reply. As I smiled down at the courageous young men, one seemed to have separated from the group. In fact he was way out in front with no look of fatigue or breathlessness anywhere upon his face or body. I narrowed my eyes further down onto the field, and a lump in my throat cut my oxygen in half.

It's was him.

I didn't know if he had a sixth sense or it was just plain coincidence that as he crossed the finish line without breaking a sweat, he glanced up to me. It was as if my whole body froze, my eyes refusing to gaze away from the almost demonic stare of those grey orbs. He gave a small, content smile before turning away and running back towards the changing rooms; the other boys still crawling towards the end. A chill snaked its way up my spine as I was broken from his control, looking back down to my number jumbled notebook. I sat on my hands once I noticed they were shaking. Did he know who I was? Did he know about me and Alex? Did he know where he was?

The question that scared me the most kept beating on the inside of my head.

What was he going to do?

I stood by my locker after school, hating the fact that some guy who might be a vampire slayer with super fast legs could sneak up on me and poke out my eyes with a wooden steak. I don't know why that particular image popped into my head, but it didn't leave my warped brain for the rest of the day. Could no one else see how creepy this kid is? It gave me shivers, and I hate that feeling.

"*Someone's walking over your grave.*" Alex joked with me once.

Alex.

I didn't care; I needed to talk to him. My house would have been impossible, it was dumpling night and those things were bigger than the stones my grandpa passed and showed us all last Christmas. It definitely put me off my turkey.

I could always make my excuses by saying I'm studying at a friend's, otherwise I wouldn't normally be allowed out on dumpling night. I think that's the reason I have ill health. Dumplings are the devils delight.

"Hey, wanna come with me to the park?" Sophie asked, nudging me back to reality.

"*Yes!*"

"Sure, but why are you going to the park in the first place?" I quizzed her, closing my locker.

"I need to stay away from home for a while, the tweevils are having their nails done straight after school and the smell from the paint gives me a headache."

I smiled. Sophie is the most normal person on this planet. Thank God she keeps my feet from stepping into cuckoo land. Oh praise the lord for Sophie and her dysfunctional family.

"Well I need an excuse to avoid family dinner tonight anyways." I replied, walking down the corridor beside my best friend. "So we can live out our misery together."

"It's a done deal."

We both laughed and left the school building. This was the perfect plan. If Alex decided to drop by, which he will because he always seems to pop up at the right moment (well, most of the time at least), he can take me back to his for the remainder of the time and at last I'll have seen his place. Oh I love it when such a cleverly crafty plan comes together.

I instantly regretted my cleverly crafty plan. It was a stupidly senseless idea, especially when it's zero degrees outside and we chose to sit on a stone bench.

"You know this is not good for my health." I wrapped my scarf around my mouth, snuggling into what little warmth it could give me.

"Haven't you had your flu jab yet?" Sophie asked, feeding the pigeons with some of Emily's leftover sandwich. Her parents don't agree with the GM content in the school dinners, so they give her some gross tasting bread. I'm surprised even the pigeons are eating that crap.

"Not yet." I sniveled, feeling my nose getting stuffed up.

"God, you should come out with a big tartan blanket around your legs." Sophie teased, taking her white earmuffs from her head and plonking them over mine.

"Ha...ha." I grumbled between sniffs. "If it was up to my mum I wouldn't leave the house without a flask and hot water bottle."

Sophie giggled as she continued tearing up the bread crumbs and throwing them a few feet in front of us. At times like these I'm grateful for my best friend's positive outlook on life. Out of all of us, she's the one who's got the most to be miserable about. Makes things like homework and extra chores seem inadequate. Boring; but inadequate.

I didn't know how many minutes or even hours had passed by, but I did know I was close to losing the feeling in my legs. Sophie seemed pretty chilly too, but she didn't complain an inch. It has been so long since we'd been able to talk like we'd had, but I could have wished for a better setting. I swear people are trying to purposely freeze me. I didn't know why, I have nothing of any value to leave in my will, except my Twilight saga. That baby is getting buried with me.

"What are you two doing out here in the freezing cold?" A soft, scolding voice interrupted my thoughts on the every so lovely Edward. I glance up to see my other sexy vampire standing beside me, with a frown. "*You especially* shouldn't be out here."

"That's my fault." Sophie piped up, chuckling. "I should have bought the hot water bottle."

"Don't you apologize." I butted in, giving Alex my most evil look. "I'm perfectly fine."

"Yeh, that's why you're sitting there like a human sized germ."

"Why you-"

"I don't think we've met." He had the nerve to interrupt my rant, holding out his hand towards Sophie. "I'm Alex."

"Sophie." My so-called best friend answered, taking his hand. "So you're the mystery guy we saw last week huh?"

"I take it she didn't tell you about us then?"

"There is no US!" I yelled, standing from my chair like a woman possessed. It was only when I opened my eyes that I noticed half the park was looking at me as if I'd just thrown up slugs.

"She this mean to *you?*" Alex raised an eyebrow.

"I know how to keep her in check." She laughed.

"Ok, shut up now." I groused, feeling my eyebrow beginning to twitch. "Before I sneeze on all of you."

"Which is exactly why I'm taking you inside." Alex responded. I opened my eyes and grinned evilly as he glanced over to my friend. "Do you wanna come with us?"

Sophie shook her head.

"I better get back home, I'm sure the smell of acrylic has left the building by now. I'll leave you two to it."

I tried to send daggers in my ex best friends back as she waved and smiled, slowly walking away.

"It must be dumpling night for you to be out here for so long." Alex suddenly piped back up. "Well, I guess I can take you to mine for a while."

My mood suddenly brightened. This day wouldn't turn out so bad after all.

Chapter 8

I didn't speak as we entered the large apartment building a few mere blocks away from the park. I didn't talk mainly because I couldn't drag my mouth up from the floor. I was too busy acknowledging the fact that Alex lived in the brand spanking new set of posh apartments that were built only a couple of years ago. That was around the same time he started stalking me. He says he was pursuing me in the name of affection. I on the other hand was close to filing a restraint against his ass. Well glancing up at my swanky surroundings, I'm glad I didn't.

"You gonna stand there catching flies or are you gonna come up and get some warmth into those skinny legs of yours?" Alex interrupted my train of thought, yet again. Next time I'll tie him to the tracks and run over him repeatedly.

"I do *not* have skinny legs." I grumbled, following him as we entered through the swiveling doors and towards the lift across the white marble flooring.

"Thunder thighs?" He asked, pressing the button.

I tried to kick him with a half frozen shin, but I get pulled into the lift before it could make contact with his groin. Pity.

As the doors close I found myself with my back against the side wall of the empty elevator, Alex's front touching mine as he looked at me with those big green eyes. Damn him and his dazzling iris'.

"Excuse me, my personal space is being intruded by some horny blood sucker and I have to warn him my knee is dangerously close to his outer male anatomy, that's if creatures of the night have any."

As I shoved him away he chuckled, leaning against the next wall with one foot on the metal behind him, hands in his pockets as he leant his head back.

"When have you seen me lurking in the shadows in the dead of midnight?" He asked.

"I wouldn't put it past you." I sniffed, turning my head away. I would have started one of my famous rants, but I decided to leave it at that. I still wanted to see his place, and judging by the number that glowed from the elevator buttons, this was going to be a treat indeed.

I was right to shut my trap. I didn't register the door closing behind me and Alex taking my coat and borrowed earmuffs from my head as I gazed around the room. It was adorned with creams and browns, leather and suede, brushed metal and dark wood. Had I walked into someone's home or a showroom?

"I should put a net over that thing." Alex grinned at my agape mouth as he walked further in, turning a corner and suddenly disappearing. I left my shoes by the door as I padded over the lush cream carpet and towards the long corner couch, diving down onto the cushy brown leather and closing my eyes. Now this is the kind of place I could only ever dream of living in. How the heck did he get this place? Does he have some sort of Vampire trust fund?

"I would say make yourself at home, but you've probably already done that." Alex's voice called from somewhere. I smiled, snuggling into the couch as my legs dangled over the arm. I turned my head and opened my eyes to the wooden coffee table sitting between where I was and the large, flat TV opposing me.

It had a book sitting upon the edge, and curiosity got the better of me as I leant over and went for it.

"Thirsty?" The unexpectedly close voice made me jump out of my skin as I soared off the couch, landing face first onto the floor.

It hurt.

A lot.

"Sleepy?" Alex teased as I sat up, cursing quietly as I turned and faced him. He held out a cup of hot chocolate to me.

"You don't drink this do you?" I asked, taking the cup between my chilly hands.

"*You* do." I do like it when he remembers little things like that. "I'm more of a coffee guy." He added, slinking down onto the couch his with own mug of steaming liquid.

"Funny, most would say you were into the haemoglobin side of things."

"What, just because my bodily functions rely on the blood of mortals mean I can't enjoy a nice cup of roasted beans every now and then?" He raised an eyebrow, taking a sip.

I sighed. I guess sticking to Vampire rules is too boring for him. As I glanced back around I realised what I was doing for before I nearly squashed my face. Picking up the book with my empty hand I studied the title.

"Bram Stokers Dracula?"

"It's quite funny to see what people think vampires are over the years." He replied. "Especially that guy, he's nuts. I mean, who on earth would want to sleep in a coffin?"

I had to laugh out loud. It seemed as though my assumptions on vampire's lives change every second I spend with Alex. Realising I was still on the carpet I placed my cup on the table and pulled myself back onto the couch beside the odd vampire. I leant back into the softness that is this heavenly suite.

"So do you sleep?"

His brow furrowed. "Probably not as much as you, but I sleep none the less."

Watching Alex I couldn't help but smile. Ok so he may be a bit annoying and tainted at times, but he's still Alex, my funny little vampire.

God, did I just say *my* vampire?

I must have blushed, because Alex laughed and rested his head on top of mine, holding onto the remote and blazing the TV to life. I exhaled deeply and relaxed, taking back my hot chocolate and letting the sounds of the plasma rush into my head. This was pure bliss.

I don't know about you, but I hate interruptions. Especially noisy ones with a mouth stuffed full of doughnuts.

"Oh hey, what are you doing here?" Ron slammed the front door shut with his foot, dropping his coat on the dining table chair and wobbling his way towards us.

"I was about to ask you the same thing." I glared back, trying not to sound put out.

"He invites himself around a lot." Alex offered an explanation from beside me, too absorbed in the chat show on TV to glance round at the new guest.

"Gees that's harsh." Ron complained, dropping into the arm chair with his bag of sugary delights.

"He'll apologize to you share that bag with me." I answered, almost drooling down my jumper.

"I will?"

"No need for a sorry." Ron sighed, extending the bag towards me. "I'm used to bouts of daily abuse."

"My hearts bleeds for you." Alex rolled his eyes as I leant over him and almost pounced on top of the delightfully smelling bag.

"Somehow I doubt that." Ron stuffed another bite into his mouth, turning to face the TV set.

After stuffing down the last morsel, I clutched my stomach, hearing its anguished cry.

"Someone's a pig." Alex looked to me.

"Someone's a bad host for not offering me dinner." I retorted, licking the sugar from my fingers.

"Funny, I thought you had to be *invited*."

"You practically dragged me over here so don't start getting smart blood boy." My eyes narrowed, prodding his front with my finger.

Ron rubbed his rotund stomach. "Yeh, I'm getting kinda hungry too."

"It's like looking after little kids." Alex sighed, standing from his seat and heading towards the phone near the door. I watched him walk away.

"Where are you going? The kitchen is that way."

"Yeh, but the pizza delivery number is over here." He answered, picking up the phone.

"Make it extra cheesy, like you."

"Haha."

"Don't forget the pepperoni!" Ron called back, his stomach growling in agreement.

I sat and nibbled at my pizza like my cousin's hamster does with a piece of carrot. It's cute, just not when it's trying to bite your finger off. I was desperately hungry, but the reason I was gnawing at the slice was because I was concentrating more on Alex.

He eats. He's a coffee drinking, pizza eating vampire. I'll never take another vampire show seriously again.

"Lemmie guess." Alex picked up another slice. "In that warped mind of yours you're thinking; 'vampires shouldn't eat!'"

My eyes stabbed into that pretty face of his.

"My voice does not sound like that."

"You should listen to yourself on tape then."

"Everyone's voice sounds different on tape."

"Excuses excuses."

"Do you guys bicker like this all the time?" Ron was watching us intently, gulping down his third slice without looking even remotely full.

"Don't all couples bicker?" Alex replied.

"Hmm, I don't recall saying I would date you." I replied smugly. "So shut up."

"So you're not dating?"

"Of course we are."

"No we are not!"

"Why keep denying it?"

"Argh you are so...."

"Yes?"

I hate it when he smiles at me; waiting for the sharp, witty comeback that I never seemed to deliver; *especially* when he looks at me like that. Argh why me?

Ok, I admitted defeat. "Go make me some more hot chocolate."

"Shouldn't your dumplings be in the bin right now?" He enquired.

"Either that or inside Peepers." I sighed. "Why, you trying to get rid of me?"

"I just don't want to get accused of kidnap." He answered. "So I'm gonna take you home."

I pouted into the pizza box.

"I haven't even seen the bathroom yet."

. . . .

I really wish Alex didn't have to run me home.

Literally.

I had to tell him to stop after a few blocks, I could feel the pizza coming back up for a surprise reunion. We continued on foot with me groaning every other minute, clutching my stomach. Dumplings would have at least made me sick by now; the pizza was instead torturing me.

"Tell me if you're gonna puke." Alex said me as we carried on down the dimly lit street.

"Why, in case I get it on your shoes?"

"No actually, I was willing to hold your hair back." He replied; a little annoyed at the fact I thought he was going to be mean. I didn't know why, I'm always mean to him and he normally reciprocates the gesture. So this time, I smiled up at him.

"You know you can be really sweet, when you want to be."

"I wish I could say the same about you."

All that newfound respect I had for him suddenly flew away again. Damn parasite. I choose to ignore him and looked ahead, but I instantly regretted my actions. I should have know that on a Wednesday night the wonderful Ella has horse riding and then has her routine of picking up Emily from her own Green peace club. The duo usually goes for pizza in the restaurant near to the hall where Emily practices her hippie life of saving the Croatian crab monkey. There they are walking straight towards us, chattering away and blissfully unaware of our approach. Thank god.

"Hey I think I'm gonna be sick." I pulled on Alex's sleeve. "There's an alleyway down here."

"Aren't those your friends?" He peered towards the talkative twosome.

"Nope, I don't think so." I tried pulling him into the alley next to us, without much success. Geez is this guy made of stone or something?

"They *are* your friends." Alex ignored my attempts to drag him away, watching my friends draw closer.

"Please don't see me, please don't see me." I repeated quietly to myself, hiding behind Alex and closing my eyes tight. As a kid I always used to think that I became invisible if I couldn't see anyone else.

"Mimi!"

Damn my five year old imaginings.

"Mimi?" He smirked over his shoulder at me. I was dangerously close to telling him where to go in a language that would make football fans close to tears.

Luckily for his ears Ella made herself known.

"Fancy seeing you here." She grinned, glancing up at Alex. "So are you going to introduce us?"

A small hole. Anywhere, a small, dark hole where no one will find me. Please.

"She's not up to much talking, she's ill." Alex piped up. "I'm Alex by the way."

"So you're the hot guy she was talking to last week." Ella smiled. Flirting is expected of Ella, even if she does have a boyfriend.

"Well Miya never told me she had such cute friends."

Hold the phone. He's flirting *back*?

"Now why hasn't she told us about such a charming guy like you before now?" Ella giggled in that sickly sweet tone of hers. I didn't care, because Alex was flirting back. He's *actually* flirting with my friend, in front of my face.

"Guess she's hiding me away from the world." He laughed. Emily must have sensed my eagerness to kick both of their behinds into next week, because she quickly drew up a plan of action.

"It was really nice meeting you Alex, but we gotta go." She pulled on Ella's riding jacket, literally dragging her down the sidewalk. "Make sure Miya gets home safe!"

"We should all meet up sometime, coffee?" Ella called after us.

"Sounds good to me!" I heard Alex call back, but I didn't see his reaction because by that time I was already half way down the street. My anger meter had gone into overload, and I was ready to explode.

"What's wrong now?"

I bumped my head onto something soft, cursing under my breath and glancing upwards. Alex looked down at me with a frown.

"You!" I growled. "I expect the girly giggles and stupid flirtations from her, but *you?*"

"Hmmm, so does this mean you're jealous?"

Now I was stumped. With one single word that bloodsucker had managed to back me into the corner of what I thought was my endless witty mind. I'm out, game over.

Well no, I did have one card left up my sleeve to leave this doofus awestruck with my breath-taking intelligence.

"Shut up."

I began to walk past him, wallowing in my achievement, but was pulled to a halt when a hand grabbed my wrist.

"I did it because I don't always know that you care about me."

My happy skip of smugness had fallen into a 1000 foot drop of guilt. I kept on staring forward, afraid of looking back and falling into a mess of crap. I probably deserve to slink down the nearest sewage pipe. Instead I simply covered my eyes with my hair, which is the only blessing this mess upon my head has given me. Suddenly I felt my legs pulled off the ground as Alex carried me away at the speed of light, a word not spoken between us as my house came into view. Had I just ruined something I never thought would end just because of my stupid stubbornness?

Chapter 9

I've always liked silence. It calms me and gave me peace of mind. Right then, it was slowly killing me. Alex placed my feet against the floor of my room, but I couldn't bear to look around at him. Instead I curled my hands into fists at my sides and glance down at my feet. Why couldn't I speak?

From behind I heard my window open once again, Alex's feet hopping onto my windowsill.

From out of nowhere I spun around and grabbed his shirt, stopping him from jumping right out of my life. Nothing happened for a few moments as I hold onto his shirt, watching his hair blowing softly in the wind that passed by the outside of my house. It was almost impossible to know what his face looked like, but I wish I did.

I couldn't take it anymore.

I pulled myself closer to him, hanging onto his frame with both hands as I buried my face into his back. I closed my eyes and prayed that this precise moment in time won't end, he won't go away. I felt myself jolt as his feet landed back onto my floor and my grip slid down his back. I often forget how tall he is, he makes me feel like a doll when I stand near him. Right then I felt more fragile than I'd ever felt in my entire live. The next movement he'd choose to make could shatter me into tiny pieces. I shut my eyes tighter, not daring to let the saltwater forming in my eyes fall.

"I'm sorry too." His voice crept into my ears, barely a whisper.

"Why? It's me who doesn't deserve you." I replied; my voice started to cave under the anger and sadness I held inside.

"Oh, it's not that." Alex answered softly. "I'm just sorry that you're using my shirt as a hanky."

I laughed, leaning my forehead on his spine whilst finally feeling the tears sloping down my cheeks.

"I'm not crying."

"You're giving my clothes a spin wash." He chuckled softly.

"I'm not." I laughed again, wiping at my face furiously. I felt his hands hold my wrists again, removing them from his back and turning himself round to face me.

"Then you're leaking." Alex placed a finger under both my eyes, wiping away the drops of water that must have escaped my harsh rubs.

"Alex I...I..."

He brought me into an embrace, resting his head on mine.

"I know you do."

I woke up the next morning half expecting to have my cover bolted around my body. I think I've subconsciously prepared for the ice storm to blizzard into my room as the window is kept open yet again. I grinned like a Cheshire cat to find that the cozy warmth I was receiving wasn't from my flower decorated duvet.

He stayed.

I was staring directly at his front, my head seeking refuge next to his chest with his breathing clear as crystal in my ears. I shuffled about in my current position and realised I still had my clothes on from last night. Well, at least he didn't try to put me in my pyjama's; I would have sleep choked him. I didn't actually remember falling asleep, just the fact that Alex picked me up and laid my down on top of my covers and then lay down next to me. We talked for hours. It was mostly meaningless matters, like the anger at my French teacher for giving me a D in my essay. I mean come on, who wants to learn how to say; "can I have some extra frogs' legs?"?

I've learnt over the time we've known each other that Alex does not open up very well. I can never get anything out of him, and I think that's why I was always so angry towards him. He knew everything about me, but I didn't know a thing about him. Maybe there's a good reason for that, but most of all I've learnt that I can't stay mad at him. Especially when he sleeps with a face like a little baby. Cute.

"You sure do stare a lot." His voice made me jump, his eyes remaining closed.

"How long have you been awake?" I frowned.

"I've learnt to wake at the slightest sound." He replied, turning onto his back as he stretched out and yawned.

"Ooh, get Crocodile Dundee." I sneered sarcastically, but I grinned as he opens one eye over to me.

"I'm better than any little lizard catcher."

"Hmm, ponder on that thought whilst I check how late I am for school." I smiled, crawling over him for my clock. I liked to keep it on my floor, that way I had more of a chance at smashing it with my foot when it rang. Finding the mechanism hiding behind the side of my bed I held it up to my eyes.

"Darn it."

"Come on, what's the damage?" I felt Alex's voice tickle onto my stomach.

"It's five in the morning." I groaned, feeling my eyelids droop.

"It's what?" He laughed, the itch on my stomach growing bigger.

"It's more sleep time." I dropped the clock back onto the floor with a slight crash, shuffling back into my warm hideaway next to Alex. "So sssh."

"I can't stay here much longer." He told me as I snuggled down. "I don't think your parents would like to see their daughter asleep with some guy."

"They never come in early." I replied, getting comfy. "I'm not much of a morning person; they've had experience with my sleepy temper."

"All the more reason I should go before you kick me out." He chuckled, leaning up from my mattress. I was going to argue, but my eyelids didn't open. His voice whispered something I didn't quite get as he left and my world fell back into darkness.

. . . .

I pondered as to why Peepers had a bathroom loafer clamped between his jaws as he trotted past me leaving the house, jumping into my dad's car. Even so, today I'm in a good mood and feel nothing can burst my bubble. Nothing can rain on my parade, nothing.

Except the rain.

I sighed heavily as I gazed out the classroom window, watching the water fall down so hard upon the pane that I could barely see outside. I was hoping for an alfresco dining experience, but sadly I was reduced to a muggy, noisy classroom feast.

"I'll trade you my chocolate bar for those macadamia nuts."

"Why on earth would you want her macadamia nuts?"

"I'm trying to cut down on the sugar; I've been putting on the pounds recently."

"Please, the only thing you ever put on is makeup." Sophie rolled her eyes as Ella began to eye her cucumber slices.

"I could get you some if you wanted." Emily offered. "My mum says they're grown in the forests of Australia, fair trade and totally organic."

"Why am I not surprised?" Ella rolled her eyes.

I suddenly heard my stomach starting to rumble, and I glanced down and frowned.

"Why aren't you eating?" Sophie accused, sounding eerily like my mother.

"Please don't tell me you're starving yourself." Ella stood up and slammed her hands down on the desk, making the rest of us jump. "For cute guy Alex?"

"No." I scowled at Ella's ridiculous nickname. My friends should know me better than that. "It's just that I left my lunch down in my locker after chemistry."

"Well you better go and get it, lunch will finish soon." Emily bit down on her swapped chocolate bar.

"It's so far away." I complained.

"Shut up and eat up." Sophie shoved my locker keys into my hands, all three of them staring at me before I caved in and slid my seat back.

The school hallways are always so empty when it's wet lunch. Everyone is always in some classroom, causing chaos wherever they choose to settle. It's kinda spooky to think of a school being quiet and empty. Ignoring the shivers tingling down my spine I carried on down towards my locker. It was a few floors down from our home room and a very long trek down various corridors. Still, at least I was getting some exercise.

Finding my rectangular shaped storeroom, I entered my key and reached in for my toasted cheese baguette and various other healthy alternatives. Mum also decided that the rest of the family had to cut back on the crap, not just our overweight dog. It didn't really bother me; I'll eat almost anything when my stomach calls out to me in anguish. Retrieving my brown paper bag I closed my locker and span quickly to head back before the bell rings.

I didn't get a chance.

A tight grip against my shoulders shoved me back against the metal, making the whole side of closets shake. I glanced up in fright at the person holding me so painfully.

The grey eyed boy.

He said nothing as he glared down at me like something possessed. I wanted to shout and scream at him, even knee him in the groin if necessary. My mind was yelling for me to fight back, but my body didn't seem to have heard. My breathing got harsh and erratic, hoping I'll suddenly wake up and realise I've fallen asleep in class again. No miracle, this was a real nightmare.

His right hand moved from my shoulder and pulled off my scarf. It whipped against my skin at the harsh speed, making me wince. His fingers were like ice, grazing down the side of my nape. His eyes settle upon the two soft bumps I carried and his lips move into a wicked smile.

"Marked." He whispered into my ear just as the bell rang, kids pouring out and into the corridors like ants. His hands suddenly removed themselves from me and he begin to walk casually away and eventually out of sight. I exhaled deeply, leaning against the lockers for support as I felt myself beginning to give way again. I wasn't worried about my crumbling kneecaps; I had a whole new bank of questions flooding my mind. The one that kept firing up the front of the queue was the one that scared me the most.

What was he going to do?

Marked?

This guy may not have known who I was, but he did know of the vampire I associated with. The tiny inkling of fear that I'd been carrying around for the past week comes back to bite me on the ass, suddenly grown into a huge ball of panic. If he'd already found me had he found Alex too? I shook my head violently, it didn't bare thinking about what this slayer could do. Well, could there be more of them? Alex said they're one huge family, so has another got to him already?

"Miya."

Hearing that voice made me cry out and turn around to face the stranger, backing away at the sudden clump of fright I'd just received. I couldn't go on like this.

"It's ok." Ron's big boned frame came into my blurry eyed view. I blinked away the tears quickly before glancing back up to the vampire. It was raining like it hadn't rained for a whole summer; my feet were soaked and cold.

"It's not!" I shout, shutting my eyes tight again as I hold onto myself tightly. I've never been like this before. "They know who I am, so they know who you are, who Alex is!"

"Who you are?" Those words were the only ones that seemed to have surprised him. I opened my eyes to his vocal reaction. His face was like death.

"Why, why does that matter so much?" I questioned, my heart lurking close to my mouth.

Just as Ron went to speak, a loud high pitched cry came from the next block down. My eyes widened so much Ron looked at me as though they would pop out and roll along the puddle infested sidewalk. I knew that voice.

"That was a child's voice." Ron whispered. I knew that, because I was on my way to pick up Jason.

Chapter 10

I'd never run so fast in my entire life. Nothing else mattered except getting to the school around the next corner. Ron grabbed my hand and I flashed around the back of the school gates like it was nothing.

"MIYA!" Came the anguished cry of my little brother, standing up from the soaking wet ground and scrambling over to me, his tear stained face and red puffy eyes barely registering inside my mind as I knelt to the ground and held him tightly to me. He was freezing cold and drenched to the bone. Glancing up from my sobbing sibling I saw Ron standing in front of me, growling like a rabid dog at the figure a few feet away. My lungs felt punctured to see the grey eyed blonde smirking, hands by his sides in clenched fists.

"Miya he said he'd hurt me!" Jason blubbered into my coat, gripping his arms around my neck like his life depended on it. "He said I wouldn't see anyone again!"

"I'm gonna slash your neck from ear to ear." Ron's voice grew deeper and I saw his eyes starting to flash a blood like red.

"Such pitiful words from a dirty beast." The boy chuckled.

My knees failed as I fell to my rear, burying my head in Jason's wet black hair.

"Anyone who associates with a vampire are just as guilty; a traitor." The blonde's eyes stilled upon me.

Ron went to move forward but the boy turned and ran through the murky playground, soon out of sight.

I felt myself become slightly more at ease, closing my eyes against my brother's head as he continued to cry into my front.

"I didn't know they'd be so low." Ron whispered, quietly, walking over and bending down beside me. "So...evil."

I felt the sobs climb my throat, clutching tighter at Jason's coat. Nothing mattered at that moment in time, everything had gone.

The sound of footsteps splashing towards us didn't deter me from my state. I was concentrating on getting Jason calm.

"What happened?" The exasperated voice came from behind me. It was the last voice I wanted to hear.

"What do you think happened?" Came Ron's slightly angry jitter, standing up from beside me.

"Miya..." His hand touched my shoulder.

"DON'T!" My voice suddenly found its way back from the pit of despair I'd only recently sunk into. His hand jerked away from me as I looked down into my brother's eyes. He looks back up at me in both fright and confusion. "You said he wouldn't harm me; let alone harm my family."

"I know I did."

"You said nothing bad would happen, you said they wouldn't find you."

"Miya I..."

"LIES!" I screamed, turning to his soaked form a few steps away from me, my eyes livid and my whole body wracked with sheer fright. "All you've ever said to me were lies!"

"That's not true."

"Then why am I sitting here with my brother so terrified he won't let me go? What would have happened if I didn't get here? What could you have possibly done?" My voice grew louder, struggling to stand to my feet as Jason's legs wrapped around my waist. My clothes were sticking to my skin and my hair matted against my back, the cold drifted through my body but I couldn't bring myself to care.

I dared myself to look Alex in the eyes. The usual green sparks had flittered away, but it just wasn't good enough for me.

"I blame myself for trusting you."

"You *can* trust me!" He replied urgently, trying to walk forward. I took a step back, keeping eye contact; rage controlling all my emotions and movements.

"NO!" I screamed, the tears from my eyes merging with the patters of rain that meet my cheeks. "Don't come near my house, don't come near my family, and don't come near me."

"I'm sorry..."

"So am I." I replied, kissing my brother's head as I turned and headed back home.

"Don't leave me Miya." Alex's voice sounded as broken as mine, but that couldn't waver my decision.

"When it was me in the danger zone, I could face it." I spoke, looking down at my brother, sniffling next to my chest and looking tired. "I'm not prepared to put my family in the same spotlight."

"Please." His footsteps edge closer but stopped as I took one last look back round to the sodden boy behind me.

"I'm not part of this anymore, I'm out."

I began to walk away, begging myself to forget those large green eyes crying out to me.

"Miya." My brother mumbled into my front. "Are we going home now?"

"Yeh." I reply. "We're going home."

I almost fell through the front door. Jason wasn't exactly heavy, but carrying him all the way back in drenched clothing and with my head slowly caving in on itself, I was exhausted. Peepers trotted in from the kitchen, sniffing our clammy bodies as I shut the door behind me with my foot. Jason still didn't want to get down. I walked into the kitchen, finding the place empty.

"Gone to Rosie and Tim's for dinner, will be back late. Lasagna is in the oven."

I'd never felt so happy to see my mother's rushed handwriting. What the hell would they think seeing us in this state?

Jason rubbed his eyes. "Miya, I'm sleepy."

"Yeh, but you're soaked." I replied softly. "You need a bath and I'm gonna give you some medicine too, we could have caught our deaths out there."

He replied with a soft nod, yawning as I dropped my things on the kitchen table and carried him upstairs, Peepers following close behind.

It was agonizingly unsettling to see Jason so silent as I washed his hair. Of course I'd done this before, but in entirely different circumstances. I washed out the shampoo and led him to his room where he pulled on his pyjama's. I walked back into my room, peeling away the clothes from my skin and pulling on my own set of nightwear. I was surprised to notice I was still standing. I turned to throw my dank clothes in the washing bin, when it catches my eye.

The red sphere with clouds that move around so beautifully slow. I felt my emotions starting to get the better of me again, so I picked it up from my desk. Walking over to my closet I threw it into one of my boxes and slammed the wardrobe doors shut.

Dinner was quiet too, watching some old re-runs of Jason's favorite cartoons as we sat on the couch and ate what little lasagna we could manage. Peepers could sense our cheerless mood; he slumped down the side of the couch as if to keep an eye on us. Neither of us was truly hungry, but if we didn't eat I knew we'd feel worse in the morning.

Tell the truth, I couldn't feel more stupid and pathetic as I did at that moment.

"Miya, can I sleep in your bed tonight?" Jason asked after swallowing the spoonful of less than tasty medicine.

"Yeh." I smiled softly, ruffling his newly soft head of hair before placing the medicine back on my desk.

He walked over to my duvet and snuggled right next to the wall as I joined him, pulling the covers right up to our faces. Jason wriggled up to me, closing his eyes and dozing off pretty quickly.

"I'm sorry." I whispered, closing my eyes tightly and wrapping an arm around his skinny back. "I'm so sorry."

I lay and sobbed quietly to myself for most of the remainder of the night. The person I hated most in this world wasn't Alex, it was me.

. . . .

Chapter 11

"So what time would you say you found your brother?"

"Who else was there?"

"What did he look like?"

The questions made my head hurt. I sat on the living room couch, the two police officers sitting on the other chairs; looking at me for an answer. I didn't have the answers, I just didn't know anymore.

I had to tell my parents. It wouldn't have been fair for me to ask Jason to keep quiet. All I did ask was that he didn't say anything whilst I lied.

"I don't know what time it was and no, no one was with me when I found him." I swallowed, holding onto the glass of water my father has handed me earlier. My mother was in hysterics, pacing around the room with Jason on her hip, mumbling sobbing apologies and hate for whoever had done this. I couldn't have told them about Ron and Alex, things would have only gotten worse. Mum and dad didn't even know who they were, and I wasn't about to add to the trouble they already had. Hopefully the cop cars outside would deter them from the house, and that guy too.

They'd kept us off school for today, though I wished I'd have gone in. I would have doubted the grey eyed guy would still be there, but I was so angry I would have killed him with my bare hands. Slayer or no slayer, he crossed the line. Alex had too.

Whether or not he knew this could have happened; he'd kept us around. I wanted to hate him with every fiber of my being, but it was slowly becoming harder and harder. I *did* hate him, but I loved him at the same time. I shook my head violently. No, no more. No more Alex.

"Is something wrong Miya?" The female officer shot me a curious glance.

"No." I replied, gripping the cushions under my legs and glancing down at the floor.

"You should have phoned us!" My mother cried. "We would have come home!"

"Don't blame Miya Lorraine." My dad replied. "She was as frightened as Jason was; at least she did the right thing with him."

I felt sick. I'd wrecked everyone's life for my own selfish reasons. I clasped a hand around my mouth, standing and running up the stairs like lightning.

"Miya!" My dad called after me, but I wasn't listening.

Leaning up from the sink I glanced at myself in the bathroom mirror. My skin was paler than usual, and I felt dizzy and weak. Why? Why did everything die?

I rolled into my room, hearing the cops talking to my parents downstairs. I had to put on a jumper, I was suddenly freezing. Opening up my closet door a strange wave of something weird hit me. I glanced down at my box of birthday cards. I've kept special ones from my friends and family every year, inside this large green box decorated with butterflies. Funny thing was; it wasn't green anymore. Taking the lid away a red light emitted out, glowing and dimming like a heartbeat.

The paperweight.

I pulled it out from its hideaway, glancing down through the glass. I suddenly jumped to find it cracking right inside my clasp. The glass looked splintered and the colour seemed to dull. Holding it in my hands I felt the throbbing from the object course through my skin.

"I don't understand this."

"Understand what honey?"

I span around to find my dad standing by my door, looking at me in a concerned fashion.

"The cold." I answered, turning back and hiding the ball back into the box, grabbing the nearest sweater I could lay my hands on.

"You ok?" He asked, moving closer as I closed the wardrobe door.

I nodded, but my dad knew. He brought me into a cuddle, kissing the top of my forehead and sighing.

"It's gonna be ok Miya, just don't blame yourself."

I closed my eyes against his front. Too late.

. . . .

7 minutes? 7 hours, 7 years?

I'm not sure how long it had been, though my mum told me I hadn't been myself for a whole week. My friends said it too and I knew that everyone was treating me differently, even myself. *He* hasn't been at school, and the police can't seem to identify this creep. I don't care; I just want my life to go back to normal again.

My dad took us to school and picked us up. He said he doesn't want a repeat of what happened so he gets the afternoon off work just to come get us. I hate being babied around, but at least this way I can't run into Alex; or Ron for that matter.

God it hurts. It hurts like nothing I've ever felt before but I have to stay strong. This whole situation had landed my family in danger, and I don't want anything like that to happen again. Even if it meant sacrificing him, I'd do it.

I dared to take another peek at the paperweight covered in birthday cards just before I went to bed. It looked even worse than it did before. I was totally and utterly confused. Why would a stupid paperweight start to break? I haven't dropped it before, and I placed it gently back into its paper home since yesterday. It almost seemed alive, like when you used to put a flower into a dark room for a few days and when you'd take it out it would be limp and almost dead. Is this paperweight a flower, or something just as fragile?

My thoughts were sidetracked as I saw something move from the corner of my eye. I raced towards my bedroom window, glancing out into the star lit sky. I swore I saw something leave my outside windowsill. As I peered around the darkened neighborhood, the paperweight in my hands started throbbing again. I glanced down, watching the red light inside going slightly bonkers. I knew I could only ask one person what was happening to this crazy thing, but I couldn't. I slumped down the side of my window and onto my floor. Life isn't fair.

I'm not sure whether it was a bad dream or just the thoughts of the past week, but I was restless. My body was dying for some sleep but my head didn't seem to agree. I tossed and turned for most of the night, trying desperately to shake loose the thoughts in my head and let my eyes close.

Impossible.

I finally forced my eyes shut and pulled the covers over my head, trying to block out any sound that probably didn't exist. God I was losing it. I even heard footsteps on my floor.

Wait.

I threw my back covers and stared through the darkness that absorbs my bedroom. There was nothing except my glow in the dark teddy bear sitting on bookshelf that caught my tired eye line.

Nothing.

So where's the red light from the enclosed paperweight?

"Sweet dreams."

That was the last thing I heard before my mind went pitch black. I thought I'd merely fallen asleep, but judging from the hard surface I woke up upon, I wasn't in my bed.

I wasn't in my house.

I wasn't safe.

M eyes finally flickered open to the image of a wooden bench underneath me.

No, wait a minute.

I sat up, groaning from the ache in my bones to get a better look. I was lying on a church pew. Flinching up in fright I glanced around frantically. I was inside a church. The stain glass windows looked empty and lifeless without sunlight, the only source coming from candles lit around the huge, bitter space. I shiver quietly to myself, holding my uncovered arms. I was still in my pyjamas, my socked feet lightly touching the stone floor underneath me.

Before I could make my move to stand, the large wooden doors at the other end of the building flung open, a body flying backwards and into the altar a few rows ahead from where I'd bolted up in terror. The mess of black hair told me immediately who it was.

"Ron!" I cried, moving to run forward.

"DON'T...move."

My head snapped around to see the grey eyed slayer walking in from the doors and down the aisle, a gun pointing directly towards me.

My eyes darted from the barrel of the weapon to a barely conscious Ron upon the cold stone steps.

"Silly girl, do you really think we've finished with you just yet?" The boy chuckled.

"I'm not with him anymore." I replied calmly, the night chill barely bothering me at this moment in time.

He held up the paperweight with his other hand, the corner of his mouth pulling up to a smirk.

"Yes you are."

Chapter 12

With each passing word my mind became even more tortured to the sounds that escaped his mouth. What did he mean?

The boy sauntered further towards us, keeping both eyes on me as he walked up to Ron, giving a swift kick into his middle. I cringed as I heard his winded cry, trying to move his shaking limbs into motion.

"Stop it." I heard myself say, staring deep into those cold, overcast eyes.

"The work needs to be done." He simply answered, his gun wielding arm as still as the night air.

"So your work is to kill?" I asked. This obviously, had been the wrong answer. The boy marched towards me, grabbing my arm before I could back away and holding the gun to my forehead. Words couldn't describe the fright that enslaved my body.

"How dare you speak ill of my work, when you cannot be saved."

I felt a pain dig itself into my side as I was thrown to the floor beside Ron. I winced, trying to hold back my anguished cry as I leant up with one hand, the other clutching my hurting region just above my hip.

"I'm...sorry." Ron turned onto his back; his eyes slammed shut from pain. "No..." I replied, managing to gain leverage on my open hand. "Don't be."

"You dare talk in the Devils whisper inside this house of sanctum?" The gun faced back down to us.

"Some house." Ron replied, leaning up. "Doesn't even have a TV."

The boy grew wild with rage, running forward and clasping his hand around Ron's throat. My eyes grew wide as he picked up the vampire from the floor, his feet not touching the stones. Ron tried to pull himself free. He's strong, but not nearly enough to set himself free.

"You filthy creatures won't have time to joke when I send you back to Hell." The boy narrowed his eyes.

Ron desperate breaths to gather air stabbed at my ears, tears starting to form in the corner of my eyes.

"Let him go!" I screamed, just about managing to stand back up. "The only vermin in here is you!"

"Miya...run." Ron heaved, his eyes slitting from lack of oxygen towards me. The boy merely turned and shot his malevolent gaze back at me.

"You..." He spoke almost in a whisper, dropping Ron back to the floor and turning to face me. "…You."

I barely had time to blink before he dropped his gun, grabbing both my shoulders and slamming me to the floor. My cries echoed off the stone pillars above before I felt his weight upon me, his face inches above mine; staring into me. Pure terror made my body stick to the floor, not daring to twitch. His hand started to graze my cheek. His touch was foreign and cold. I began to cry, wishing I would wake up.

"You're worse than him." He spoke almost normally, eyes covering every inch of my face. "You chose to share your pure human life with a wicked soul, which makes you tainted and dirty."

None of his words truly enter my mind; my head was too full of fear to even think about that matter of fact tone he used with me.

"Even the prettiest flowers will share their nectar." His mouth moved to my ear, his whisper making my whole body shiver.

A suddenly impact made me blink twice, feeling the weight leave me as the boy suddenly slammed further down the church way, his landing echoing off the steel pipes of the organ in the furthest corner of the building. A warm, familiar pair of hands wrapped themselves around my body, pulling me up to a sitting position. I gaze up into a set of gemstone eyes. My whole body warms to the embrace that he gives me.

"I'm sorry." He whispered, holding me tight.

. . . .

I couldn't help but clutch onto the form I'd missed for so long, too long. My tears ran silently down my face, leaning into his front.

"I'm never gonna leave you again, you hear?" He told me, his head resting next to mine.

"Yeh." I replied, my voice barely a squeak. "I do."

Alex lifted me up, cradling me for a while as I watched his eyes gaze down the church aisle. They narrowed.

"It's not over yet." He spoke softly, placing my feet back upon the ground.

"No, far from it."

Another faster than light motion set my eyes ablaze. I felt Alex's hand being snatched away from mine as he shot back down a church pew, the boy pinning him down against the splintered wood that now surrounded them.

"Alex!" I screamed, looking on in desperation.

With a kick to the middle the slayer blasted over a few pews, wood raining down around them.

"Run." Alex seethed, standing back up, his eyes beginning to fill with red. "Run and don't you dare look back."

Before I could even being to object the slayer threw himself back at Alex, the two becoming involved in a brawl I could barely keep up with. I know one thing, I was not running.

The glint that caught my eye turned my head to the solid metal gun that lay upon the floor a few feet away from an unconscious Ron. I ran faster than I'd ever run before kicking away the weapon and kneeling beside Ron, pushing his slumped body to life.

"Wake up!" I cried desperately, begging him not to be dead. "Please Ron, please!"

After a few heart in mouth moments the Vampire's blue orbs wrenched open, a groan escaping his mouth as he began to sit up once again.

"Where..." He gazed around the church, witnessing the two in a mind numbing fight across the battered oak seats.

"He came." I answered his face, trying to move him into a more comfortable position.

"Did you honestly doubt him?" Ron looked back to me, a soft smile upon his face.

I smiled back, but only for a split second as the bone crunching sound of a body slamming against ten tons of rock rocketed into my eardrums.

No.

"ALEX!"

His body lay like a rag doll behind me, struggling to move his head from the floor.

As if on instinct I ran towards him, but I was pulled back by an almighty force clamping around my neck, chocking the wind out of me as I'm dragged down the altar steps and away from the recovering Ron. I felt my fingers forced around the trigger of the gun, moving in the aim of Alex a few metres away.

"You shall do it." A hoarse voice fell into my ear, his breath erratic and deep. "You shall murder the honey bee."

Chapter 13

It was as if I'd had an outer body experience. I felt as if I was in a dream world, or even one of my brother's video games. I could just unplug the socket and the screen would grow blank, it would be over.

Not now, this was the terrifying reality that I was faced with.

"No!" I cried, trying my best to move my arm away from Alex's direction. His grip around my neck only tightened, causing me to yelp from the amount of weight pressed upon my throat. My arm wasn't moving; it was still facing Alex.

"You'll do it." The boy chuckled. "Then you'll kill him." He moved our arms towards Ron, before turning to face my heart. "Then you'll repent your sins and send yourself for God's judgment."

My whole body wracked, the gun facing back out at Alex. My eyes widened, making contact with his aching body as he pulled himself up the wall and onto his feet once again. The red of his eyes leaked from his brown hair, staring indefinitely towards us.

I felt the catch click upon the gun, taking aim straight for Alex's chest.

"The only way to kill a vampire is to shoot his heart." The grey eyed monster told me, his voice sending shivers down my spine. "So take aim."

"No!" I sobbed, trying to fight back.

"You're right."

I stopped almost automatically, listening to the slayer's unlikely choice of words. His heart? A heart is something that's in your body and pumps blood around. How can his heart be anywhere else?

But....he's not human. So, what he's saying...it could be true! Still if that's the case...

Where is his heart?

I felt my arm pulled out towards my right side. My eyes left the strangled look upon Alex's face and found the next target.

Impossible.

The red aura swallowed my eyes as I gazed upon the object helplessly.

The paperweight.

"He never told you, did he?" The slayer whispered into my ear like a poisonous snake. "He never let you in on his precious little secret."

My eyes darted back towards Alex standing against the wall, his breathing deep as his gaze met mine. He looked so regretful; I could barely see him blink.

"You've been doing me a favor." The harsh voice continued to penetrate my mind. "His strength has depleted, his agility decreased and his power almost gone. He hasn't fed in a while that's why, but also because you broke that insufferable heart of his."

My eyes didn't stray from Alex, realising that all my stubbornness and naivety made this happen. If I didn't see Alex ever again, I would have killed him.

"I'm sorry." I whispered to him.

"Don't worry." I heard the gun click from inside my palm, his fingers gripping mine against the trigger. "You'll be with him again soon."

I watched my finger beginning to close around the trigger, my whole life seemed to have broken down inside of the emeralds I can't help but gaze into. He looked back at me, an emotionless face. Ron was right, I'm not strong. I'm so pathetically weak I didn't see past my own concerns.

"You're not weak Miya." His voice carried down the church aisle like a soft melody that soothed my heart. My watery eyes looked up from the cold metal gun encased into my hand and back to Alex. "You were never weak; I want you to know that."

Everything was blocked from me except Alex's weary frame against the church wall. It was a heart wrenching punishment.

He gave a soft chuckle.

"Love you, rice valley."

Wait.

Something inside of me woke up; something inside of me telling me that it wasn't mean to end like this.

"An unlikely choice of last words." The slayers tongue rasped on the inside of his mouth. "I'll have to cut out your demonic throat."

No.

"NO!"

I heard the sound of a single gunfire as the world formed into chaos around me. The sound of smashing glass stopped my lungs from exhaling.

What was happening?

Chapter 14

The large shards of the stain glass window collapsed quickly onto the church floor, letting moonlight glitter into the edifice like a natural spotlight. Multicolor strips of pane flash past my eye line as I feel myself being set free. A sudden rush of heat flew past me, pulling the slayers grasp away from my neck and into the collection of candelabras in the far corner near to the door. The smack of the metal gun colliding with the floor grabbed my lost attention. My fingers reached to grasp it until a foot crunched down onto the evil contraption.

"That thing wasn't meant for humans hands." Ron stood over me, gazing down at the broken pieces of steel with pure hatred inside of his ocean blue eyes. "Come on."

His hand extended down to mine as I grabbed on for dear life and felt my thinly covered feet breach contact with the floor.

"You might wanna take better care of this." He held up the paperweight, still full and red. My fingers clasped around it like a lock. I wasn't going to let this precious package leave my sight again.

Still, the sight that next welcomed my eyes will be one that stays with me for the rest of my life, however long that may be.

From the eerie darkness a figure stands, his eyes oozed the darkest red and blood dripping down his hand and his shirt. The black strained my eyes, but I daren't look away. Those orbs suddenly turned back to the priceless emeralds, round and alive. He glanced my way, a soft smile upon his lips. I smiled back, gripping the ball tight.

"Let's get you out of here." Ron sighed, wincing in pain as he leant down.

"You're not strong enough to carry me." I replied, moving us away towards the pews for support, my sleepiness becoming deeper with each passing second.

The glide of another's hands wrapping around my shaking body lifted me from my barely standing position. I gazed up at Alex, looking down at me with tranquility written upon his dirty, moist face.

"Can you walk?" He asked Ron. The wounded vampire replied with a simple nod, catching his breath.

I felt my eyes beginning to sag as he walked down the church aisle towards the doors.

"Pfft, I've had enough of this freaking 'run for you lives' crap." He grumbled, rubbing a seemingly sore shoulder. "Can we please retire to the tropics now?"

"You've still have Slayers to contend with." Alex replied, passing through the doorway, the old creaky hinges almost squeaking a good riddance. "They'd be in floral shirts."

"Hey, do you think I'd look good in shorts?"

I laughed almost suddenly, emitting the last little bit of energy I had.

"Well, at least someone is looking on the bright side." Alex chuckled, the vibrations tingling on my skin.

I smiled contently, leaning into his arms. "Take me home; I need some freaking sleep."

The last thing my eyes saw was their faces, a calming aura around their skin.

The last thing I heard was the faint sound of a midnight wind, cool and crisp.

The last thing I felt was Alex's warmth feeding mine.

The last thing I touched was the small ball within my grip, the glass smooth against my calloused hands.

Chapter 15

"She's fine, just sleep deprived."

"You sure she didn't get hurt?"

My eyes opened blearily, a mess of colors. Still, I felt wonderfully warm to even wonder who was inside my bedroom. I wasn't like I couldn't guess.

The warm, silky voice chuckled; a sudden figure looming over me with eyes a shocking crimson. "Alex; she'll be fine. However, your concern seems to have woken her up."

I sat up with great effort, feeling a pair of hands guide me into a comfortable position. I rubbed my eyes, glancing towards the warmth that plonked itself beside me. "Where am I?"

"In your room, duh?" Alex rolled his eyes, a mighty Cheshire cat stretching across his cheeks.

Ah my room, how good it was to be back home; and not dead. Still, I frowned. Alex was being like this because he felt staggeringly guilty; but didn't want me to see it. His guard was up; much like mine has been before.

"Don't stay up too long." The silky voice glided into my thoughts. "You have a slightly high temperature; I would advise some serious bed rest."

I looked to the side of Alex. There stood a man who couldn't have been more than forty years old, with wonderfully shiny black hair and those red jewels set inside of his seemingly angelic face. Not a wrinkle in sight, just perfectly tanned skin.

Pfft, course he was a vampire.

His lengthy frame stood up straight, grasping a leather suitcase beside his grey trench coat.

"Now if you don't mind; I have some 'batlings' to feed, if you catch my drift." He smiled, nodding a subtle goodbye before turning towards the open window. I must have blinked, because he was gone.

"Dr. Park." Alex answered my priority question. "I asked him to come and check on you."

"I'm fine." I frowned deeper, looking into his eyes.

Alex cocked his head. "Yeh, I know that *now*."

I sighed, letting my body lean into his as I closed my eyes. "Where's Ron?"

"Home." He replied, wrapping his arm around me. "Probably conked out by now."

"Hmm." I murmured, too involved in his scent to register his answer. I could feel sleep overcoming me again; I didn't want to fight it.

"Go to sleep." He whispered, sliding us down the mattress and pulling the duvet around me tight.

"Will you stay?" I asked, gripping his shirt.

I couldn't almost picture his quaint smile. "Yeh, I'll stay."

Then I fell asleep; at home, in bed and desperately in love.

I woke up with an almighty headache, and no Alex in sight. Instead I felt another hand resting upon my forehead, with brown flicks of hair tickling my nose.

"Hmm, Miya you don't look so good." My mother spoke, sitting softly beside my feet. "Did you leave that window open all night? You could have caught your death!"

Damn bat.

. . . .

For the rest of the week I was reduced to my bed, watching Jason's favorite cartoons whilst he chose to selflessly keep me company. I'd learned that he had an abnormally large head.

Surprisingly my mum and dad were so concerned about me they even rang the doc. *Human* doc mind. Luckily he confirmed I only had a small case of the flu; not that I had almost been killed by a crazed psychopath. God bless practitioners.

Luckily through that week I kept myself occupied by reading the daily newspaper. A dead body found in a church had sparked major gossip within the town, and the police were completely baffled. They now believe it's all connected to the incident with Jason and are still keeping the case open. Good luck with that one.

The boy's name was Silver. No one ever came forth claiming to be his family. It hadn't said how he died; but I had already taken a pretty accurate guess. It was finally confirmed he bled to death.

I went back to school on a good note. The girls couldn't have been gladder to see me, judging from the fact that they wouldn't leave my side for the rest of the day. That's what you call good friends.

. . . .

"Ok, bathroom check."

"We just went half an hour ago!"

"A girl has to keep her beauty in check." Ella winked towards Emily. She merely sighed and shook her head, following the blonde down the steps from the school roof on which we sat upon.

"Fancy witnessing another trowel session?" Sophie joked, bending down beside me as I gazed up at the clouds.

"Nah, go ahead." I replied, my hair whipping around my face. "It'll be good to get some silence for a while."

Sophie giggled and stood up to follow the others. I continued watching the sunny sky for a moment longer, before smiling and closing my eyes.

"I knew I should have taken that restraining order out on you."

"You think that would have stopped me?" Alex's chocolate voice replied. I opened my eyes and turned round to see the Vampire walking towards me, hands in pockets. "How are you feeling?"

"Pretty good." I replied, looking out across the city view. "Damn quacks have me on the drip every other night, but I can't complain."

"That'll be a first."

"Alex." I sighed. "Shut up and pull me up."

I held out my hands and chuckling the brunette obeyed, pulling me to my feet so that my face was against his chest.

I hate being small.

"New start." He told me, his emerald eyes gazing down at me.

"Uh huh." I answered. "Unless there's any more vampire chums hiding around?"

"You'd be surprised." He laughed.

"Well, I'm only interested in this one." I smiled, my hands playing with the buttons on his shirt.

"Sorry, was that a *nice* comment that left your mouth?" Alex raised an eyebrow. "I should have got that on tape; I doubt I'll hear it again."

I sighed in frustration. "Get *this* on tape."

I grabbed his collar, pulling his lips down onto mine as I stood upon my tiptoes to reach him. I probably would have melted into a puddle of romantic goo if Alex hadn't wrapped an arm around my waist, the other running through my hair. As we parted I looked up to his eyes, our faces still touching.

"I think I'll replay that." He smiled, reaching back down.

As we stood there like idiots, I pondered something. Life is always going to be full of surprises, but I guess you got to take each day as it comes. Though knowing this guy, surprises are bound to be of the demonic, blood sucking kind.

I'm looking forward to it.